CATULLE MENDÈS (1841–1909) was a French man of letters and the protégé of Théophile Gautier, whose daughter, Judith, he married, though their relationship did not last long. In 1860 he founded *La Revue fantaisiste*, publishing such authors as Villiers de L'Isle-Adam and Charles Baudelaire. He gained the reputation as a sensualist after his 'Le Roman d'une Nuit,' which appeared in the same review in 1867, was condemned as immoral, and he was sentenced to a month's imprisonment and a fine of 500 francs for publishing it. He wrote voluminously—plays, poetry, essays, novels, and short stories. Friedrich Nietzsche dedicated his *Dionysian-Dithyrambs* to Mendès, celebrating him as "the greatest and first satyr alive today—not just today . . ."

BRIAN STABLEFORD has been publishing fiction and non-fiction for fifty years. His fiction includes a series of "tales of the biotech revolution" and a series of metaphysical fantasies featuring Edgar Poe's Auguste Dupin. He is presently researching a history of French *roman scientifique* from 1700-1939 for Black Coat Press, translating much of the relevant material into English for the first time, and also translates material from the Decadent and Symbolist Movements.

CATULLE MENDÈS

BLUEBIRDS

Translated and with an Introduction by

BRIAN STABLEFORD

THIS IS A SNUGGLY BOOK

ISBN: 978-1-943813-25-4

CONTENTS

INTRODUCTION

*L*ES OISEAUX BLEUS by Catulle Mendès, here translated as *Bluebirds,* was first published Victor-Havard in 1888. It was, in essence, a slightly expanded version of *Les Contes du rouet* [The Spinning-Wheel's Tales] (1885), adding three new items—the first three—and omitting only one, "Vieilles chansons d'Alsace" [Old Songs of Alsace], which is not a *conte* but a rather disorderly collage of vignettes. In fact, the first and third of the additional items are not modeled on tradition folktales either, the first being a sentimental contemporary story and the third, like one of the items retained from the earlier collection, being a satirical allegory. Even so, the collection is more nearly a specialized collection of pastiche folktales than the earlier *L'Amour qui pleure et l'amour qui rit* [The Love that Weeps and the Love that Laughs] (1883) and *Pour les bells personnes* [For the Fair Sex] (1886), although both are dominated by that kind of material, and a few more had been included in the more varied *Lesbia* (1886). Numerous other items of a similar kind were included in later, usually more generalized, collections of short fiction, including *Pour lire au bain* [For Reading in the Bath] (1888), *La Princesse nue* [The Naked Princess] (1890), *Pierre le véridique* [Honest Pierre] (1890), *Le Confessional: contes chuchotés* [The Confessional: Whispered Tales] (1890), *Le Bonheur des* *autres* [The Happiness of Others] (1891) and *Le Chemin du coeur* [The Way to the Heart] (1895) but none of those collections retained a celebrity equal to *Les Oiseaux bleus*, which was only overtaken in popular esteem by one of the longer stories that Mendès wrote in a similar vein, the classic *Luscignole* (1892). Selected stories from *Les Oiseaux bleus* were reprinted in a number of samplers of Mendès' work, including *Contes choisis* [Selected Tales] (1897).

The tales contained in the collection are interesting, not only because they illustrate a particular evolution within the pattern of the author's own works, but because that pattern reflects a more general one associated with the evolution from the French Romanticism of the first half of the nineteenth century to the Decadent and Symbolist Movements of the *fin-de-siècle*. Catulle Mendès (1841-1909) was one of the key figures in the latter phases of that process of development, launching his literary career in the 1860s under the patronage of Théophile Gautier, whose daughter Judith he married—much against her father's wishes—in 1866, and then becoming a leading figure among the "Parnassians" who attempted a renewal and revivification of Romantic ideals, before he entered wholeheartedly into the Decadent Movement launched in the 1880s. The stories in the present collection extend—though not in the order of their presentation—over a linear spectrum, moving by degrees from the affected sentimentality of Romanticism to a darker and somewhat jaundiced world-view that illustrates the Decadent sensibility very well, although all the stories were written in advance of the enormous fashionability that the sensibility in question achieved in the late 1880s.

The complex evolution of the French literary *conte* went through one of the crucial phases of its evolution in the seventeenth century, when collections of reconfigured folktales and imitations thereof began to appear in several European nations, and sparked a fad in the literary salons associated with some of the leading ladies of Louis XIV's court. Perhaps inevitably, given the sexual politics of the day, it was a male writer, Charles Perrault, who eventually claimed center stage in popular attention, and was hailed as the archetypal exponent on the new genre, in a collection of six moralistic fantasies initially published as *Contes de ma mère l'Oye* (1697; tr. as *Tales of Mother Goose*) but the genre obtained its most familiar label from the near-simultaneous collection of works by the far more prolific and considerably more sophisticated Marie-Catherine Le Jumel de Barneville, Baroness d'Aulnoy, *Les Contes de fées* (1697), who was the real star and promoter of salon literature of that sort. The salon writers deliberately employed and exaggerated the elements of the *merveilleux* in such traditional tales, in calculated flagrant defiance of the dawning "Age of Enlightenment" that ruled such material superstitious, obsolete and unworthy of credence.

The nearest English equivalent to the French word *féerie* is "enchantment," and *fées* are, strictly speaking, enchantresses (as in the enchantress of Arthurian legend known in English as Morgan le Fay), but the title of Madame d'Aulnoy's first collection was translated into English as "fairy tales," thus foisting that label on an entire genre of subsequent English fiction, most of whose included stories do not, in fact, feature "fairies" as previously defined and deployed by such influential domestic writers as William Shakespeare and Edmund Spenser. Although Mendès' stories do routinely feature individuals very similar to the fairies of previous English literature and art—

and take some inspiration directly therefrom—I have nevertheless preferred to translate his "fées" more directly as "fays."

Because the genre defined by Madame d'Aulnoy was adapted, following Perrault's precedent, to a principal role in children's literature, which it still holds, and because versions of many particular tales reprocessed by d'Aulnoy, Perrault and others retain central roles in that usage, it is sometimes forgotten that the production of such tales in the French salons was intended for the amusement of adults. Then again, any versions that had ever circulated orally were probably a good deal more cynical, satirical and erotic than those eventually adapted by Perrault's followers specifically for the amusement and for the "*civilization*" of children. Although many of the stories in the present collection could plausibly be read to or by children, most require an adult understanding to perceive and appreciate their use of the apparatus of enchantment to express a poignant disenchantment, and that essential irony lies at the heart of the exercise.

Although some of the stories composed by the seventeenth-century salon writers were based on pre-existing tales, most were original compositions. Many of them, however, fed back into oral tradition, becoming archetypal examples of "fakelore." Catherine Bernard's "Riquet à la Houpe" (tr. as "Ricky of the Tuft") was plagiarized by Perrault, and was thus added to the standard repertoire of "traditional tales," along with material he adapted from Madame d'Aulnoy, while Mademoiselle de La Force's "Persinette" was subsequently collected by the Brothers Grimm as an ostensible German folktale, under the title "Rapunzel." Perrault added one story to his collection that he made up himself, "Le Petit chaperon rouge" (known in English as "Little Red Riding Hood"), which subsequently became one of the most prolifically reprocessed tales ever written. Many of the composers of salon *contes* did not, therefore, retain the credit for their inventiveness, but some of it proved remarkably enduring, and they laid groundwork for the extension of the tradition of literary *contes* not only throughout the eighteenth century but long thereafter. The ironic sophistication of the elements of the *merveilleux* begun by the salon writers eventually provided the foundations for an important genre identified by twentieth-century French critics and literary historians, the *fantastique*: a genre recognized in France some time before American and British critics and historians began to delineate "fantasy" as a genre.

The renewal of the tradition of *merveilleux* in the nineteenth century was greatly assisted by the championship of such work by one of the French Romantic Movement's most ardent promoters, who founded the first of the *cénacles* that became the Movement's own specialized salons, Charles Nodier. Nodier's most celebrated ventures in "fakeloristic fantasy," including the classic *Trilby* (1822) and *La Fée au miettes* (1832; tr. as *The Crumb Fairy*) are novellas rather than *contes*, but their example assisted nevertheless in prompting the production of many shorter works by writers associated with his own *cénacle* and its various spinoff groups, including those hosted by Théophile Gautier and Delphine de Girardin.

Nodier's influence in France was, however, combined and significantly supplemented by that of writers associated with the German Romantic Movement, who adopted a far more earnest approach to the materials, some of them proposing that the essential *volksgeist* [folk-spirit] of the German people could be found in its folklore, and that it could be reproduced, renewed and sophisticated in the production of *kunstmärchen* [art-folktales] such as those composed by Ludwig Tieck, the Baron de la Motte Fouqué and Wilhelm Hauff. French writers were never able to take such materials as seriously as their German counterparts, and their work always remained lighter, often deliberately flippant, but the shadow of the German endeavor was nevertheless there, and even in reacting against it, the French material began to take on some of its pretentions to profundity, its writers occasionally turning back the edges of their velvet gloves to offer a glimpse of clenchable iron fists within.

The fact that Catulle Mendès became one of the most prolific writers of fakeloristic *contes* has much to do with the fact that he was a thoroughly professional writer, always eager to exploit the scope provided by the *feuilleton* slots of newspapers even though he was not at all suited to writing the interminable serials that were the normal fare of the slots in question. As the plethora of story collections he published in the 1880s and 1890s readily illustrates, Mendès was one of the first writers to begin methodically adapting short fiction to fit into such slots, active in that regard some time before a handful of the newspapers of the late 1880s began making a point of dedicating one of their slots—some papers had two, or even three—to short fiction.

Mendès realized very quickly that the fakeloristic *conte* offered one of the few fictional frameworks readily adaptable to that purpose, and thus became one of the earliest writers to establish a virtual production-line in order to mass-produce work of that sort. *Les Oiseaux bleus* contains the early produce of the line he developed with that purpose in mind, and illustrates the manner in with he developed and sophisticated the method, providing significant exemplars in that vein, which numerous other writers followed. Mendès also played a significant role in the development of naturalistic short fiction and erotic fiction adapted for the same market slots, including the *contes cruels* that were later to play such an important role therein, and there are significant overlaps between his various production lines adapted to the same marketing strategy.

Because the fashionability of short fiction declined over time by comparison with the prestige of the novel, Mendès is now primarily remembered, to the extent that he is remembered at all, for his novels, several of which continued to be reprinted in the twentieth century while most of his collections were not—a fate that also overtook many of his contemporaries. There is no doubt, however, that he had a particular fondness for *contes de fées*, and during a crucial phase of his own early evolution as a writer, even though he won greater fame as a poet and dramatist, they were an element of his literary production that he considered precious. Although at least two of his other collections mostly consisting of material of that kind also warrant translation, and another could easily be assembled by selecting the relevant items from his more varied collections, this translation of *Les Oiseaux bleus* is the most logical starting-point for such an enterprise.

❦

This translation was made from the copy of the Victor-Havard edition reproduced on the Bibliothèque Nationale's *gallica* website.

Brian Stableford

BLUEBIRDS

THE EVENING OF A FLOWER

IT had been thrown during the fête from carriage to carriage; launched at hazard, caught and thrown again, it had been like the shuttlecock of those exquisite rackets that are the hands of Parisiennes; then, an idler having fumbled it, it fell into the mud, amid the short damp grass. No one, at first, had paid any heed to it, and subsequently, in the rain-soaked fête, a thousand feet trampled it beneath the languid gaiety of Chinese lanterns and colored glass, while the big drums and trombones of the fairground booths sounded. It was a very small pink eglantine, almost still a bud, with a long thorny stem.

As I was passing through the crowd yesterday evening, I saw a little pale redness in the gray mud, which was that dead flower. Immediately, I divined what the fate of the eglantine had been, triumphant and then melancholy during the day of pleasure and folly. Now it was there, a memory, between two little heaps of mud as if between two pages of a book, already withered but still charming, a soiled and perfumed relic. I thought of picking it up, of keeping it; how did I know whether I might not find the odor that is dear to me among all, the odor that I have aspired for a single minute with my rapid lips, at the extremity of a little gloved hand, in an antechamber, after five o'clock tea, while coats were being put on? Then again, that rose was all that remained of the gaiety of an hour, of the beribboned and florid promenade, in which Paris had imitated the fantasy and laughter of an Italian Corso. The poet who passes by has a duty to collect what remains of human joy, the sadness that is like the lees of happy things; and afterwards, he makes verses of it.

I therefore bent down to pick up the flower.

But a hand had anticipated mine: a very small hand, that of an ill-dressed little girl, sordid and almost ragged, with the appearance of a beggar. I let the child do it, and did not dispute the morose wreck that she seized, which she put into her corsage, in the gap in the fabric devoid of buttons, very quickly and furtively. Poor little thing! It pleased her, habituated as she was to walking in the mud, to pick a flower there.

But I observed the people—a man and a woman—who were with the child, and I followed them, among the hubbub of all those people making haste under the rain. They were poorly dressed, he in a jacket, she in a wool-en dress without a mantle. The disorder of a loosened chignon hung down over her neck; he had brown hair, curled by a suburban hairdresser, beneath a round hat. They both displayed in their costume and their attitude an abandonment of poverty, a dilatoriness of rags. That Parisian couple, the lout and his female, was truly frightful. She did not give him her arm; they made the little girl who had picked up the flower walk ahead of them; and as they walked, they talked.

It was a bitch of a day, all the same, because of the still-menacing downpour. Rich people had not quit their carriages, and with the bourgeois who had come to see in

4

spite of the bad weather there was nothing to be done; they were cunning, and took good care of their pockets. No, it was maddening, after all, not being able to get out of trouble when one has a real desire to work and is no more one-armed than one's comrades. Foreigners have all the luck, the English especially, because of the Grand Prix; people take them for respectable folk who have relatives in the stables; people chat with them in order to get information about the horses that are running, and they, while chatting . . . but the French suspect the French; no means of engaging them in conversation. In sum, it is now ten o'clock in the evening, they came to the fête at two in the afternoon, and in all that time, not one windfall, nothing; they wouldn't even have had enough to take a glass before bedtime if the child hadn't got a few sous begging between the carriages. If that wasn't enough to make one angry! In order to live, then, was it necessary to go abroad, since there was no means of plying one's trade honestly in one's homeland?

And all that was said in grunts, with filthy oaths and the drinking-den accent that gives all speech the ignominy of argot.

Why did I follow, why did I listen to, those vile pedestrians? Because of the little girl, all in rags, thin, ugly and paltry. What was exquisite was that she had picked up a flower.

"Marguerite!"

"Maman?" said the child, with a start.

The mother gave her a slap.

"Next time, answer more quickly. Here, look, there in front of us, those people coming. Go on, then, hurry."

The child approached a bourgeois family, almost running in the rain, in quest of a carriage, and, extending a hand, in a falsely tearful voice, whined: "Messieurs, Mesdames, we're five children in the house. Papa is out of work. It'll bring you luck!"

She was given a two-sou piece which, when the people had passed by, she handed to her mother.

"Stupid!" said the latter. "You should have run after them, they'd have given you more." And she gave her another slap.

The child dissolved in tears. She could not have been more than seven or eight. So thin, she had beneath the glare of the illuminations an almost deathly pallor, with patches of redness that looked like splashes of mud. And she wept with brief sobs. Then she resumed marching in front of the hideous couple, no longer weeping, her hand on her corsage. One might have thought that it consoled her to touch the flower she had picked up.

What could it be to her, that flower? Born in some dirty house in a populous city, habituated to a life without Sundays, she could not have had any nostalgia for fields, bushes, and running through woods with comrades on emerging from school; an eglantine for her, must have been something sold to gentlemen in the evening on the boulevards—and then, if the taking had not been good, slaps on returning home after midnight. All day long, during the fête, she had seen a crazy exchange of bouquets between coupés and victorias; well-dressed, splendid, happy ladies, their faces flushed with joy, laughing and ducking their heads to avoid the collision of the flying roses and poppies with their hats.

Hatred of flowers—flowers that were a métier for her and luxury for others—that is what she ought to have experienced, that poor creature. But no, she was still palpating, under the buttonless fabric, the eglantine she had picked up; and, her eyes scarcely dried, she had a smile on her lips: a pensive and resolute smile, with an air of glad premeditation, as if she had formed the design of some great joy.

I noticed that she had a torn and poorly folded newspaper under her left arm. Once, it fell, and she picked it up very quickly. What did she want with it? I looked at her. Sickly and sad, she was not, however, unpleasant, Washed and well-dressed, one could have made a beautiful rich child out of that ugly poor child. She walked with a firm tread. She had something in her eyes that resembled a dream.

Meanwhile, the man and the woman, with me still following them, had left the fête. They had reached I know not what suburban avenue. They stopped under a floating awning, heavy with rain, and sat down at a table. I stopped too, and sat down not far away. They asked for a bottle of wine. I saw them under the light of an Argand lamp hanging on a stake. Their faces, his hairless and hers moustached, were repulsive. Leaning on their elbows, they talked in low voices, with a conspiratorial murmur. Around us, people who must have been stable-hands and jockeys' valets were making a great racket, shouting for the waiter, quarreling and insulting one another. There was an odor of stables in the air, along with the odor of wine-casks. I noticed that the lout and his mate were glancing from time to time, while making signals, at two valets in liveried waistcoats who were playing cards, with small coins on the table.

But where was the child?

Close by, sitting on the ground, between people's feet.

And it was a charming sight.

Of the old torn newspaper she had made two little paper carriages—carriages, or their vague resemblance—and her hands, sometimes here and sometimes there, were throwing from one carriage to another the flower that she had picked up a little while ago, the eglantine salvaged from the short damp grass.

I understood then why she had seized the melancholy wreck so rapidly, why she had kept it so carefully. There, between the legs of the drinkers, in the foul air, feet in the mud, skirt in the mud, crouching down, she was imitating, for herself alone, all the gaiety and faded glory of the fête.

She was catching and throwing, in a single faded eglantine, the thousand bouquets of the youthful battle, and she was amusing herself, and laughing; and she had, that little beggar, that child of thieves, that ragged creature—while the man and the woman, leaning over red glasses, were plotting some evil deed—she had, more sincerely, on her heart and her lips, all the joy of beautiful socialites exchanging blossoming grapeshot.

Soon, she would go home to some obscure, stinking hovel where she would sleep badly, during the drunken quarrels of her father and mother. But no matter; the little wretch would have had the illusion, for a moment, of being happy, like so many magnificent ladies.

And it was, I thought, by virtue of the pity of destiny that the pink eglantine, almost still a bud, with a long thorny stem, had fallen from an awkward hand into the grass, amid the mud.

THE BEAUTY OF THE WORLD

IN those days, in that country, the girls and young women, if they knew that they were pretty, only knew it by hearsay. Scarcely hung on a wall or taken in hand, all mirrors, large or small, shattered into luminous debris without any evident impact, as if of their own accord. And do you know why they broke in that fashion? Because they were in despair at not being the mirror in which Princess Amarante reflected her flowery lips and, beneath her sun-gold hair, her sky-blue eyes.

For a hundred leagues around, even by searching for a long time, one would not have encountered a lady or a damsel who was comparable for beauty with the princess. She was the enchantment of everything that surrounded her, humans, animals and things; her little dog could not weary of admiring her, any more than her father the King. If she went an hour without traversing the room where the gentlemen of the court were, they became ill with sorrow; if she did not go for her accustomed stroll in the park, the balsams and the hyacinths, as they went to sleep in a rustle of foliage, said to one another, even after the most beautiful day: "How somber the weather was today."

But she was at least as nasty as she was beautiful; having profound blue eyes that softened delightfully in the light did not prevent her from entering into fits of anger that made everyone tremble; she more often had a desire to bite than to smile, even though her mouth had the loveable softness of a little rose-bud.

And anger was not her greatest fault; she was envious —she, who possessed so many diamonds and pearls in caskets of jade and gold—to the point of going pale with rage if she saw one or two drops of dew on a matinal primrose, or a few glass beads around the neck of a pauperess.

On top of that, her heart being closed to all tenderness, she had reduced to despair the most handsome and richest princes on earth, who had been unable to see her without falling in love with her; a dozen suitors were cited who had allowed themselves to die of the chagrin of having been unable to obtain her hand in marriage.

❧❀❧

Once, when she was playing blind man's buff on the lawn with her maids of honor—it was a game fashionable at court at the time—she overheard two pages walking in a nearby pathway behind a syringa bush, talking about a marvelous bird that resembled, according to travelers' tales, a furnace of pink gems in flight, and which had its nest on the highest summit of a rugged mountain in the land of the Algonquins.

Immediately, although she had, in twenty aviaries, hoopoes, hummingbirds, cardinals, amethysts, emeralds, parakeets, brown and pink finches, wrens the color of fire, birds of paradise and nightingales, she wanted the unknown bird. She summoned a prince who, for love of

10

her, had been staying at the court for over a year, in great melancholy. He was the nephew of the Emperor of Trebizond; he was as young and handsome as a spring morning; in order to please the princess, he had accomplished the most perilous exploits and had triumphed over the rudest ordeals, but she had only ever recompensed him with rejections of the love and devotion that he never ceased to testify to her.

When the prince arrived, she said to him: "Seigneur, you will go, if you please, to find me the bird like a furnace of pink gems that has its nest in the Algonquin Mountains, and, if you bring it to me, I might perhaps allow you to kiss the nail of my little finger."

"Oh, Madame," cried a maid of honor, "don't you know that in its distant solitude, that bird is guarded by a thousand ferocious eagles with iron claws and beaks? They would soon tear to pieces, even if he were the strongest and most courageous of living men, anyone who was insane enough to approach them."

Amarante had already broken, with a furious hand, the stem of the nearest rose-bush.

"Why are you interfering, Mademoiselle?" Then turning to the prince, she said: "I thought, Seigneur, that you had already gone."

He bowed and withdrew at a rapid pace. Such was his bravery, and such, above all, was his desire to merit the promised recompense, that he triumphed over the thousand ferocious eagles. Not many days had gone by—perhaps the mountain was less distant than people believed—when he reappeared, with the marvelous bird made of living gems on his fist, like a tame falcon.

11

With a disdainful expression, the princess declared that the little winged beast was not worth the reputation that had been credited to it, although she condescended to caress it two or thee times. Cruel and forgetful, however, she did not give her rosy fingernail to the nephew of the Emperor of Trebizond to be kissed, and did not even notice that the vanquisher of eagles had a lacerated forehead, cheeks, neck and hands, still covered with blood. He withdrew without complaint, resignedly.

※ ※ ※

And that was not the only peril to which she exposed the prince. Because she desired a peerless emerald, he was obliged to descend into the entrails of the earth and triumph over a multitude of gnomes armed with flaming torches. He came back smoking all over from burns. The princess was willing to accept the fine stone, but of the promised little finger there was no question.

Another time, she demanded that he go and pick for her, in the domain of a greatly feared enchanter, a flower that sang like a nightingale, although the flower bloomed in a clearing in an immense forest of which all the branches were jutting spears. He came back pierced by a thousand thrusts, pink with wounds, almost dying. The princess consented to listen to the song of the flower, but refrained from saying to the Emperor's nephew: "Here is my rosy fingernail."

And he made no complaint, perhaps glad to suffer, even without recompense, always sad and meek, for her, who was so cruel.

One morning when she was playing Baguenaudier[1] in a gallery with her maids of honor—it was a game that was no less fashionable at court than blind man's buff, in those days—she heard two officers of the palace talking behind the curtain of a door about a young woman more exquisite than all women and all fays; an African giant was keeping her captive in a bronze castle. She was so perfect that she was simply known as the Beauty of the World, to express that there was no one beautiful but her on earth. And the officers, thinking that no one could hear them, added that Amarante, compared to that young person, was merely plain.

Four Chinese vases shattered into smithereens beneath the furious small fists of the princess. A living person prettier than her was something she could not tolerate! The idea immediately occurred to her of making the person who had the strange impudence to prevail over her in beauty perish amid the most frightful tortures.

She summoned the nephew of the Emperor of Trebizond.

"Seigneur," she said, "you will go, if you please, to fetch me the Beauty of the World, whom an African giant is keeping captive in a castle of bronze, and, if you bring her back, I swear that, this time, I shall not refuse your lips the rosy fingernail of my little finger."

"Oh, Madame," cried a maid of honor, "don't you know that in that distant castle, the Beauty of the World

---

1. The French *baguenaudier* is commonly used to mean "time-waster," but with reference to a "game" it refers to a kind of puzzle also known as the Chinese Rings or the Devil's Needle.

is guarded by a thousand warriors with the heads of lions and tigers, who tear apart and devout, in less time than it takes a vulture to crunch a skylark, any insensate individuals prowling around the vicinity? An innumerable army of heroes brandishing lightning-bolts instead of spears couldn't vanquish those monsters, which never sleep! The prince is doomed, if he doesn't refuse to obey your caprice."

Amarante slapped the overly compassionate maid of honor on both cheeks, and then turned to the prince.

"What, Seigneur! You haven't come back yet?"

He bowed his head and went out. But it was only after an absence of several months that he showed himself again before the princess, while she was traversing the courtyard of the palace.

He was in a state that would have moved the most atrocious of hearts to pity. His clothes were hanging off in ragged strips; profound bites furrowed all of his flesh; one of his arms was missing—he had doubtless left it in the maw of one of the warrior with the head of a lion or a tiger. But with the pride of victory brightening his eyes and floating in his scattered hair, he was superb and magnificent! And behind him, among black slaves, on the back of an elephant, there was a palanquin of yellow velvet, with long gold fringes.

"Be blessed," said Princess Amarante, "if you have brought the Beauty of the World."

"I've brought her."

"In that palanquin?"

"Yes."

"Hurry up and get her down!"

The prince approached the elephant, which knelt down, and, the yellow velvet having parted, those who were present saw within it, all snow and gold, such an admirable individual that they were dazzled, as one is when one looks at the glory of the sun.

Princess Amarante uttered a cry of joy and rage, so glad was she to have in her power, in order to make her a victim of her hatred, the woman that humiliated her by means of such an incomparable beauty. And, either because her horrible contentment disposed her to some forbearance toward everything that was not the Beauty of the World, or because she finally could not help admiring the obedience and the victorious bravery of the prince, she exclaimed:

"Seigneur, it's not only my little finger but my entire hand, my entire person, that I shall give to you in exchange for the Beauty you have conquered. You shall be the king of my realm and the husband of my bed!"

Already she was making a sign to the officers and servants to bring the prisoner to her.

But the prince said: "I have indeed, conquered the Beauty of the World, Madame—but I have conquered her for me, not for you, for my love, not your hatred. Because your barbarity has too often refused me your little finger, after so many labors in which you have risked my life, I do not want your entire person, and I am taking this woman to my palace in Trebizond, who is more beautiful than you, and who is as kind to me as you are cruel."

With that, he climbed into the palanquin, whose curtains closed again and the enormous elephant, as swiftly as the nimblest antelope—for it was, I think, an enchanted elephant—disappeared in the sunlit dust of the road, while Princess Amarante, in order to get over her rage, bit the arms and shoulders of her maids of honor with her beautiful teeth.

THE LUCKY FIND

THE clerk in the lost property office did not manifest the slightest astonishment when, having raised the panel of his little window, he saw facing him, in the black and yellow corridor, a young man as handsome as a spring dawn, clad solely in a golden quiver slung over his shoulder and a crimson blindfold over his eyes. The young man was not alone, for he had a lady by his side, with the best figure in the world, who would have appeared completely naked had she not been clad in the lilies and roses that were blooming in her skin; but she had a star of diamonds in her hair.

The clerk, as I said, did not manifest any surprise; it would not have been worth the trouble of being an old Parisian if it were necessary to be astounded by anything.

So, he looked at the newcomers with an expression that testified to the most perfect indifference, and asked, professionally:

"Have you lost something?"

"Yes," replied the young man clad in a quiver.

"Yes," replied the young woman dressed in her pink and white skin.

"Your clothes, perhaps?"

"I've never had any."

"Would I not have been wrong to have any?"

The clerk grunted: "Get to the point; I don't have time to waste in dialogue. What have you lost?"

"I am, as you can see, Amour . . ."

"Indeed!"

"I am, as you can see, Beauty . . ."

"Indeed!"

"We've lost," they said, "the respect and adoration that the human race had avowed to us."

"Hmm! Hmm! Those are things that it will doubtless be difficult to recover. Let's think about it, though. Have you any memory of the times when this misfortune overtook you, and the places that you went?"

The god and the goddess tried in vain to hide their embarrassment.

"Many days have succeeded one another, and I've been seen in more than one place," he said, "since I quit Cytherean soil for the city that stands in the vicinity of Bougival and Asnières."

"It isn't yesterday," she said, "that I emerged from the waves beneath the modesty of my hair, and it has been a long time that I have been resident in the capital known as Paris."

"I've spent my nights in the boudoirs of illustrious socialites and unimportant sluts."

"I haven't disdained to show myself at balls, at fêtes, backstage in theaters and café-concerts."

"I've sworn a thousand oaths, which I haven't kept, at the feet of many amorous women."

"I've offered myself, and I've given myself, many times, in evenings of caprice and stormy lassitude."

"I've debased myself, for the pleasure of caresses, to the extent of forgetting sane jealousies, and the sacrilegious acceptance of sharing."

"I've sold myself for necklaces of pearls and amethysts, and for banknotes with heaps of gold."

The clerk exclaimed: "Damn it! That's a fine way to carry on! Persons as considerable as you ought to have shown more restraint, and not acted so irresponsibly. Admit it, it's really your own fault if you've lost the respect and adoration of the human race; and between us, I don't really believe that you'll get them back. Do you think that even the most disinterested of coachmen bring back objects of that sort? Oh, if you lived in the provinces, in small towns or villages where pure betrothals are eternalized, you'd have some chance of getting back what you lack, but in Paris, after so many adventures . . . but after all, it's necessary to see; take the trouble to wait for me for a moment. I'll go make a search."

They waited for a long time, because the clerk was an infinitely conscientious man. He looked on all the shelves, in all the drawers and all the cupboards.

He saw opera-glasses that had coveted the layered skirts of dancers and the palpitations of breasts in the cleavages of low-cut dresses, fans behind which the hypocrisy of kisses had promised eternal tenderness, and mirrors that had reflected the greasepaint of lying lips. He saw, in wallets lost by clubmen, checks that would have been cashed in smiles, and, in purses lost by young women, gold coins solicited during two gasps of ecstasy. And in the pell-mell of so many and various things, there were virtues and modesties found on the cushions of cabs, forgotten in the rooms of lodging houses, dropped in the gutter of some side-streets, where the hook of some rag-collector had picked them up along with other debased innocences. There were also the virginities of children cast to the ignoble concupiscence of old men, which the maidservant of some brothel-keeper had swept up the next day. But the honest clerk could not put his hand on the respect and adoration that Amour and Beauty had lost, and he returned to his little window and said:

"You can put on your mourning-dress, you know; we don't have what you need."

Then Beauty and Amour displayed the most extreme desolation. What was the point, for her, of being the charm and splendor of eyes, and what was the point, for him, of being the only dispenser of unique intoxications, if the esteem and fervor of souls drew away from them henceforth? They were divinities scorned by their priests! You can understand that the situation was somewhat distressing.

"What do you expect me to do about it?" said the clerk, with his pen behind his ear. "You ought to behave like honest deities."

But a loud voice, rude and benevolent, shouted: "Come on, come on, don't despair, damn it! There's a remedy for everything."

The man who had just come into the yellow and black corridor was one of the Company's coachmen. He had a big nose, an enormous mouth and the expression of a cheerful drunkard. He was doubtless bringing some object that had been forgotten in his vehicle.

"Yes," he went on, "I want to get you out of trouble. Do you know what I picked up just now on my cushions? Here, look! Behold the illusions of a poor little girl, as fresh as the flowers and as pretty as the birds, who climbed into my fiacre yesterday, very joyful, with a handsome lad who had his arm round her waist . . . but she was weeping when she got out.

"Illusions, which make you believe all lies, which make you see stars in a pitch black sky and roses in midwinter— take them, take them away, I'll give them to you.

"Make a gift of them to humans, fill their eyes, their hearts and their heads with them, and believe me, the entire race of mortal imbeciles will surround you with respect and adoration—you, Amour, as if you'd never soiled yourself with treasons and debaucheries, and you, Beauty, as if, an angel ignorant of private rooms, you'd never, with your leg outside your bloomers and a little flesh above the garter, ablaze in the gaslight, tipped off the hat of a dazzled provincial with the toe of your little boot!"

THE DREAMING BEAUTY[1]

THERE is not only the story that is written thought-
lessly; there is also the legend; and it is necessary to
recognize that it has frequently happened to the most
conscientious and best-informed story-tellers—Madame
d'Aulnoy, and the worthy Perrault himself—not to relate
things exactly as they transpired in the land of Faerie.
Thus, the older of Cinderella's sisters did not wear to
the prince's ball, as has previously been believed, a red
velvet costume with English trimmings; she had a scar-
let dress embroidered with silver and fringed with orfray.
Among the monarchs of all lands, invited to the wedding
of Peau d'Ane, some did, indeed, come in sedan chairs,
others in cabriolets, and the furthest travelers mounted
on elephants, tigers and eagles, but the storyteller omitted
to inform us that the King of Mataquin made his entry
into the courtyard of the palace sitting between the wings
of a tarasque[2] that expelled the flames of precious stones

---

1. The original title of this tale, "La Belle au bois rêvant," is a calculated variation of Perrault's "La Belle au bois dormant," which is
usually translated into English simply as "The Sleeping Beauty." As
the wood is essentially irrelevant, I have followed the same principle
of abbreviation.
2. A tarasque is a Provençal chimera, famously featured in one of the
most popular French legends of the saints, the story of Saint Martha.
Mendès was by no means the only French writer to employ the term

through its nostrils.

And don't imagine that you can catch me out by asking me from whom and in what manner I was enlightened on those important points. I once knew, in a thatched cottage on the edge of a field, a very old woman, old enough to be a fay, and whom I always suspected of being one. As I sometimes came to keep her company when she was warming herself in the sun in front of her little house, she conceived an amity for me, and a few days before she died—or returned, her time of ordeal having ended, to the mysterious land of Vivianes and Melusines—she gave me as a farewell gift an exceedingly ancient spinning-wheel, which was most extraordinary, for every time one rotates the wheel, it starts speaking or singing in a soft, slightly quavering, voice like that of a chatty and cheery grandmother.

What the voice relates is a great many lovely stories, some that no one knows and others that it knows better than anyone else; and in the latter case, as it is not lacking in malice, it takes pleasure in pointing out and rectifying the errors committed by the people who have involved themselves in writing those stories. You can see that I have a reliable source, and you would be quite astonished if I told you all the things that it has revealed to me.

For example, you imagine that you know in all its details the story of the princess who, having pierced her hand with a spindle, fell asleep so profoundly that nothing could bring her out of her slumber—not even *eau de la reine de Hongrie*[1] with which her temples were rubbed—and

---

in preference to the commonplace "dragon" in his *contes*, and I have retained the term wherever it features in the present collection.

1. *Eau de la reine de Hongrie* is a kind of perfume, originally made in

who was laid down, in a castle in the middle of a park, on a bed embroidered with gold and silver. I'm sorry to tell you that you don't know at all, or know very imperfectly, the conclusion of that adventure; and you would undoubtedly remain ignorant forever if I didn't make it my duty to inform you.

Yes, yes, the spinning-wheel purred, the princess had been asleep for a hundred years when a young prince, driven by amour and glory, resolved to reach her and awaken her. The great trees, the horns and the brambles drew apart of their own accord to let him pass. He marched toward the castle, which he saw at the end of a long avenue, and went in. What surprised him a little was that none of his followers had been able to go with him, because the trees had drawn together again once he had passed.

Finally, when he had traversed several courtyards paved with marble—servants with bulbous noses and vermilion faces were asleep beside their cups, which still contained a few drops of wine, providing sufficient evidence that they had fallen asleep while drinking—and when he had followed long hallways and climbed stairways where guards were snoring, their rifles shouldered, he found himself in a completely gilded room. There he saw, on a bed whose curtains were open on all sides, the most beautiful spectacle that he had ever seen: a princess, who appeared to be fifteen or sixteen years old, whose resplendent glamour had something luminous and divine about it.

---

the fourteenth century from rosemary crushed in alcohol, so-called because the wife of Charles Robert of Hungary, Elisabeth of Poland, was exceedingly fond of it. It was popular in Louis XIV's court, where it was a favorite of Madame de Sevigné and Madame de Maintenon. The name is still employed on a more sophisticated product marketed by Fragonard.

I'll grant that things happened like that—it is still the spinning-wheel who is speaking—and that the author, up to that point, hasn't lied with too much effrontery. But there is nothing more false than the rest of the tale, and I cannot admit that the awakened Beauty looked at the prince with an amorous gaze, or that she said: 'Is that you, Monseigneur? You've been awaited for a long time.'

If you want to know the truth, listen.

The princess stretched out her arms, raised her head slightly, half-opened her eyes, closed them again, as if frightened by the light, and sighed deeply, while Pouffe, the little dog, also awakened, yapped angrily.

"Who has come, then," the god-daughter of the fays eventually asked, "and what do they want with me?"

The prince, on his knees, exclaimed: "The person who has come is the one who adores you and who has braved the greatest perils"—he was boasting a little—"in order to extract you from the enchantment of which you have been captive. Quit that bed, where you have slept for a hundred years, give me your hand, and let us return together to the light and to life."

Astonished by that speech, she considered him, and could not help smiling; for he was a very well-made young prince, who had the loveliest eyes in the world, and spoke with a very melodious voice.

"It's true, then?" she said, parting her hair. "The hour has come when I can be liberated from my exceedingly long sleep?"

"Yes, you can."

"What will happen to me if I emerge from the shadows and come back among the living?"

"Can't you guess? Have you forgotten that you're the daughter of a king? You'll see your delighted people running to meet you, uttering cries of pleasure and waving banners of every color. Women and children will kiss the hem of your dress. In sum, you'll be the most powerful and most fêted of the queens of the earth."

"It would please me to be a queen," she said. "What will happen then?"

"You'll live in a palace as brilliant as gold, and when you climb the steps to your throne you'll walk on mosaics of diamonds. The courtiers grouped around you will sing your praises; the most august foreheads will incline before the omnipotent grace of your smile."

"To be praised and obeyed would be charming," she said. "Shall I not have other pleasures?"

"Chambermaids as adroit as your godmothers the fays will dress you in robes the color of the moon and the sun, powder your hair, and put beauty-spots on the edge of your eye or your mouth; you'll have a great cloak of golden cloth trailing behind you."

"That's nice!" she said. "I was always something of a coquette."

"Pages as pretty as birds will offer you selection-boxes full of the finest delicacies and pour into your cup the sugared wines whose perfume is so sweet."

"That's very good!" she said. "I was always something of a gourmet. Will those be all my joys?"

"Another delight, the greatest of all, awaits you."

"Oh! What's that?"

"You will be loved."

"By whom?"

"By me! If you don't judge me unworthy of pretending to your tenderness . . ."

"You're a good-looking prince, and your costume suits you very well."

"If you deign not to reject my wishes, I will give you all my heart, as another realm of which you will be the sovereign, and I shall never cease to be the grateful slave of your most cruel caprices."

"Oh, what happiness you promise me!"

"Get up, then, dear soul, and follow me."

"Follow you? Already! Wait a minute. There's doubtless more than one tempting thing among all those you offer me, but do you realize that, to obtain it, I would have to abandon something better?"

"What do you mean, Princess?"

"I've been asleep for a century, it's true, but for a century, I've been dreaming. I'm also a queen in my dreams, and of what a divine realm! My palace has walls of light; for courtiers I have angels who celebrate me in music of an infinite sweetness; I walk over scattered stars. If you only knew what beautiful robes I put on, and the unparalleled fruits that are put on my table, and the honeyed wine in which I steep my lips! As for amour, believe that I have no lack of it, for I'm adored by a spouse more handsome than all the princes of the world, faithful for a hundred years. All things considered, Monseigneur, I don't believe that I'd gain anything by emerging from my enchantment; I beg you to let me sleep."

With that, she turned toward the wall, pulled her hair over her eyes again, and resumed her long slumber, while Pouffe, the little dog, stopped yapping, and was content, with its muzzle between its paws.

The prince went away, crestfallen. And since that time, thanks to the protection of the good fays, no one has come to trouble the Dreaming Beauty in her slumber.

26

THE MALADROIT WISH

BAREFOOT, his hair in the wind, a vagabond passed along the road, in front of the king's palace. Quite young, he was very handsome with his golden curls, large dark eyes and mouth as fresh as a rose after the rain. As if the sun had taken pleasure in gazing at him, there was more light and joy on his rags than on the satins, velvets and brocades of the gentlemen and noble ladies grouped in the court of honor.

"Oh, how pretty she is!" he exclaimed, stopping suddenly.

He had perceived Princess Roselinde, who was taking the air at her window—and truly, it was impossible to see anything on earth as pretty as her. Motionless, with his arms raised toward the casement as if toward an opening in the sky through which paradise was visible, he would have stayed there until nightfall if a guard had not chased him away with a thrust of his halberd and harsh words.

He drew away, lowering his head. It seemed to him now that everything before him and around him was somber: the horizon, the road, and the trees in flower; since he could no longer see Roselinde, he thought that the sun was dead.

He sat down under an oak tree on the edge of a wood and started to weep.

"Hey, child, why are you so sad?" asked an old wood-gatherer who emerged from the forest, her back curbed beneath a heap of dead branches.

"What's the point of telling you? You can do nothing for me, old woman."

"In that you're mistaken," said the old woman. At the same time, she straightened up, throwing off her burden. She was no longer a wood-gatherer, but a fay as beautiful as the daylight, clad in a silver robe, her hair garlanded with flowers and gems. As for the dry branches, they had taken flight, covering themselves with green leaves, and, having returned to the trees from which they had fallen, they were full of singing birds.

"Oh, Madame Fay," said the vagabond, falling to his knees, "have pity on my misfortune. For having seen the king's daughter, who was taking the air at her window, my heart no longer belongs to me; I sense that I shall never love any other woman but her."

"Well," said the fay, "that isn't such a great misfortune."

"Can there be a greater one for me? I shall die if I cannot become the husband of the princess."

"What prevents you from becoming her husband? Roselinde is not betrothed."

"Oh, Madame, look at my rags, my bare feet; I'm a poor child who begs on the roads."

"No matter! The man who loves sincerely cannot fail to be loved; that is the eternal and tender law. The King and Queen might reject you scornfully, and the courtiers mock you, but if your tenderness is true, Roselinde will be touched by it, and one evening when, having been chased away by servants and bitten by dogs, you are weeping in some barn, she will come, blushing and happy, to ask you for half of your bed of straw."

The child shook his head; he did not believe that such a miracle was possible.

"Be careful," said the fay. "Amour doesn't like people to doubt his power, and he might punish you in a cruel fashion because of your lack of faith. However, since you're suffering, I'd like to come to your aid. Make a wish and I'll grant it."

"I'd like to be the most powerful prince on earth, in order to marry the princess I adore."

"Oh! Without going to so much trouble, why don't you sing a love song under her window? Anyway, since I promised you, it shall be as you desire. But I must warn you about one thing: when you've ceased to be who you are now, no enchanter or fay, even me, can return you to your original condition; once you've become a prince, you'll be one forever."

"Do you think that the royal husband of Princess Roselinde could ever desire to beg for his bread on the roads?"

"I hope you'll be happy," said the fay, with a sigh.

Then she touched his shoulder with a golden wand, and, in an abrupt metamorphosis, the vagabond was a magnificent lord, dazzling in silk and jewelry, riding a Hungarian stallion, at the head of a cortege of plumaged courtiers and warriors in golden armor who were blowing into trumpets.

※❦※

Such a great prince could not be poorly received at court; he was given the most insistent welcome. For a week there were, in his honor, tournaments, balls and all the fêtes imaginable. But it was not those pleasures that occupied him! At every hour of the day and night he thought about Roselinde; when he saw her, he felt his heart overflowing with delight; when he heard her speak, he thought he was hearing divine music, and he almost fainted with pleasure once, when he gave her his hand to dance a pavane.

One thing distressed him slightly: the woman he loved so much did not appear to pay any attention to the cares he rendered her; most of the time she remained silent, with a melancholy expression. He persisted nevertheless with his project of asking for her hand in marriage, and, as can be imagined, Roselinde's royal parents did not refuse such a considerable suitor. So the former vagabond was to possess the most beautiful princess in the world.

Such an extraordinary felicity troubled him to the point that he responded to the King's consent with extravagant gestures scarcely compatible with the solemnity of his rank, and it would not have taken much to make him dance a pavane on his own before the entire court.

Alas, that great joy was of short duration. Scarcely had she been informed of the paternal determination than Roselinde fell, half dead, into the arms of her maids of honor, and when she came round it was to say, while sobbing and wringing her hands, that she did not want to marry, and that she would kill herself rather than wed the prince.

⁂

More desperate than can be expressed, the unfortunate lover precipitated himself, in spite of etiquette, into the chamber to which the princess had been transported and fell to his knees, extending his arms toward her.

"Cruel woman!" he cried. "Retract those words, which are murdering me!"

She opened her eyes slowly, and replied, languidly but firmly: "Prince, nothing will triumph over my resolution; I will never marry you."

"What! You have the barbarity to lacerate a heart that is entirely yours! What crime have I committed to merit such a punishment? Do you doubt my love? Do you fear that I will cease one day to adore you? Oh, if you could read within me, you would no longer have that doubt or that fear. My passion is so ardent that it renders me worthy even of your incomparable beauty; and if you do not allow yourself to be moved by my plaints, I shall only find a remedy for my woes in death. Give me hope, Princess, or I shall die at your feet."

He did not limit his speech there; he said all the things that the most violent dolor can inspire in a smitten heart, so well that Roselinde allowed herself to be moved by it, but not in the fashion he had desired.

"Unfortunate Prince," she said, "if my pity, for want of my tenderness, can be a consolation to you, I grant it to you willingly. I am all the more able to pity you because I am enduring myself the torment that is distressing you."

"What do you mean, Princess?"

"Alas, if I refuse to marry you, it is because I love, hopelessly, a vagabond who passed in front of my father's palace one day, barefoot, his hair in the wind, and who looked at me, and has not come back!"

ISOLINE-ISOLIN

IT happened one day that two fays met on the edge of a forest near a large city. One of them, whose name was Urgande, was in a very bad mood because she had not been invited to the baptism of the King's daughter, but the other, whose name was Urgèle, was experiencing all possible satisfaction because she had been invited to that great rejoicing—and among the fays, as among humans, one is good when one is content, and malevolent when one is upset.

"Why, good day, my sister," said Urgèle.

"Good day, my sister," growled Urgande. "I suppose you've had a great deal of pleasure at the home of your friend the King of Mataquin."

"More pleasure than I can say! The rooms were so brightly illuminated that I could have believed I was in our subterranean palace, where the walls are gemstones and the ceilings sunlit crystal; the most delicate dishes were served on golden plates, on lace tablecloths; into cups shaped like lilies, wines were poured so perfumed and so sweet that I thought I was drinking nectar from flowers; and after the meal, young men and beautiful damsels, so light and so well-dressed that they might have been mistaken for birds of paradise, danced the prettiest dances in the world."

"Yes, yes, I could hear the violins from here. And doubtless, in recognition of such agreeable hospitality, you gave the little princess, your god-daughter, very precious gifts?"

"That goes without saying, my sister. The princess will be as beautiful as the day; when she speaks, it will be like the song of a warbler; when she laughs, it will be like a blossoming rose; in sum, there are no perfections of which I did not make her a present, and when she is of an age to be married, she will espouse a prince so handsome and so loving that none will ever have been seen so charming and so infatuated."

"A marvel!" said Urgande, grinding her teeth. "I too would like to show my generosity to your god-daughter."

"Oh, my sister, don't make her some fatal gift! Don't pronounce some fatal speech, which you'll never be able to retract! If you'd seen the little princess in her cradle, so dainty and so frail, like a little bird without feathers, if she had smiled at you with her eyes the color of cornflowers and her mouth the color of eglantines, you'd be utterly charmed, and wouldn't have the heart to do her any harm."

"Yes, but I haven't seen her! She will, therefore, be as beautiful as the day, since no fay can prevent what another fay has resolved; she will have a voice as sweet as a warbler and her lips will blossom like a rose; she will marry the most handsome and loving of princes; but . . ."

"But?" repeated Urgèle, full of anxiety.

"But as soon as she is married, on the very night of the wedding, she will cease to be a girl and will become a boy!"

You can well imagine that the good godmother was

33

frightened by that prophecy. She pleaded and she begged, but Urgande did not want to hear it, and plunged into the earth with a snigger that frightened all the birds in the forest. Urgèle continued on her way, head bowed, wondering how she could protect her god-daughter from such a disastrous accident.

⁂

At sixteen years of age, Princes Isoline was so beautiful that all over the world there was talk of nothing but her beauty; those who saw her could not help adoring her, and those who did not see her were smitten with her anyway because of the publication of her renown. In consequence, ambassadors came from all lands to the court of Mataquin to request the hand of the princess for the richest and most powerful monarchs.

Alas, the King and the Queen, alerted to the future promised to their child, were unable to reply; it would have been imprudent to give in marriage a damsel who would be so strangely metamorphosed on the night of her wedding. They sent away the ambassadors very respectfully, without consenting or refusing, as apologetic as it was possible to be.

As for Isoline, who had been left in ignorance of her cruel destiny, she cared very little whether she was to be married or not; her innocence did not worry about that. As long as she was allowed to play with her doll and her little dog in the pathways of the royal garden, where the birds said to her: "Your voice is sweeter than ours," and where the roses said to her: "We are not as rosy as your lips," she was satisfied, and did not ask for anything else.

She was like a little flower, unaware that it ought to be picked.

One day, however, when she was knotting a convolvulus stem around the neck of her little dog, which was yapping with pleasure, she heard a great noise in the road nearby. She looked up, and saw a magnificent cortege on the march toward the palace, and, at the head of the cortege, on a white horse shaking its mane, there was a young lord, who looked so fine, so splendidly handsome, that her sight was dazzled and her heart troubled.

Oh, how lovable he is! she thought; and, thinking about such things for the first time, she admitted that, if his intention was to ask for her in marriage, she would not experience any displeasure.

Meanwhile, the young lord, looking over the hedge, had perceived Isoline. He stopped, also charmed.

"May the good fays grant that you are the daughter of the King of Mataquin," he exclaimed, "for I have come to espouse her, and there is nothing on earth as charming as you."

"I am Princess Isoline," she said.

They said no more, still looking at one another; from that moment on, they loved one another with a tenderness so ardent that there are no words to express it.

꧁꧂

Imagine the predicament in which the King and Queen found themselves! It was not to ambassadors, this time, that it was necessary to respond, but to their daughter herself, begging, weeping and swearing that she would fall ill if she were not married to the man she loved, and would surely die of it.

On the other hand, Prince Diamant was not one of those people that it is easy to fob off; he was the son of the Emperor of Golconda, he could put four or five armies in the field against his enemies, any one of which would have been sufficient to ravage several kingdoms; there was, in consequence, everything to be feared from his anger, and it could not fail to irritate him greatly if the hand of princess were refused to him. To inform him of the frightful fate reserved for Isoline would not resolve the difficulty; he would not have believed such an implausible story, and would have believed that he was being mocked.

In consequence, softened by their daughter and frightened of the prince, the King and Queen began to wonder whether it might not be as well to let matters take their course as if no disaster would result therefrom. It might also have been the case that the fay Urgande, after so many years had renounced her vengeance.

In the end, not without many hesitations, excuses and delays, they consented to the marriage of the two lovers, and there had never been seen, even in a royal wedding, a more beautiful bride or a happier groom.

※❦※

To tell the truth, the King and Queen were far from feeling tranquil; after the celebration, when they had retired to their apartment, it was impossible for them to sleep. They feared that at any moment they might hear screams, doors broken down, and see the prince appear mad with despair and fear.

But nothing troubled the nocturnal calm; they were gradually reassured; doubtless they had been right to think that the malevolent fay had retracted her prophecy.

The day after the wedding, they went into the throne-room without overmuch anxiety, where the newlyweds would not take long to come, in accordance with custom, to kneel beneath the royal and paternal blessing.

The door opened.

"My daughter!" cried the King, full of horror.

"Isoline!" moaned the mother.

"No longer your daughter but your son, Father! No longer Isoline but Isolin, Mother." And, so saying, the new prince, charming and proud, his sword at his side, turned up his moustache with a challenging expression.

"All is lost!" said the King.

"Alas!" said the Queen.

But Isolin, turning toward the door, said in a soft voice: "Come on, my dear Diamantine! Why are you trembling like that? I'd hold your blush against you, if it didn't make you more beautiful."

For, at the same time that the princess had become a young man, the prince had become a young woman; it was thus, thanks to the good Urgèle, that the vengeance of the malign fay was thwarted.

THE MIRROR

IT was in a realm where there were no mirrors. All the mirrors—those that were mounted on walls, those that were held in the hand, and those that were carried in the purse—had been smashed, reduced to smithereens on the order of the Queen. If the smallest looking-glass had been discovered in any dwelling whatsoever, it would not have failed to cause the inhabitants to perish amid the most frightful tortures.

As to the motives for that bizarre caprice, I can tell you what they were. Ugly to the point that the worst monsters would have appeared charming next to her, the Queen did not want to be exposed, when she went into the city, to the risk of encountering her image, and, knowing herself to be horrible, it was a consolation to her to think that at least others could not see their own loveliness.

As you can imagine, the girls and young women of that country were not at all satisfied. What was the point of having the most beautiful eyes in the world, a mouth as fresh as a rose, and putting flowers in one's hair, if one could not consider the eyes, mouth or coiffure in question? As for going to see their reflection in streams and lakes, it was necessary not to count on it; the streams and pools of the country had been hidden beneath carefully-joined flagstones; water was drawn from wells so deep that it was impossible to see the liquid surface, and not in buckets in which there would have been scope for reflection, but in almost-flat ladles.

The desolation, therefore, went beyond the imaginable, especially in coquettish young women, who were no rarer in that land than in any other; and the Queen had no sympathy for them, being content, on the contrary, to find almost as much pleasure in their being unable to look at themselves as she would have experienced fury in seeing herself.

⁂

There was, however, in a suburb of the city, a young woman named Jacinthe who was slightly less chagrined than the rest, because of a lover that she had. Someone who finds you beautiful and never tires of telling you so, can take the place of a mirror.

"What? Really?" she asked. "The color of my eyes has nothing that can displease?"

"They are like cornflowers into which a bright drop of amber has fallen."

"I have no dark patches on my skin?"

"Know that your forehead in purer than the glitter of snow; know that your cheeks are like pale but dewy roses!"

"How ought I to think of my lips?"

"That they are similar to an open raspberry."

"And of my teeth, if you please?"

"That grains of rice, no matter how fine, are not as white."

39

"But with regard to my ears, have I not grounds for disquiet?"

"Yes, it is disquieting to have, amid light, fluffy hair, two small shells as complex as newly-bloomed carnations."

It was thus they talked, her charmed and him even more delighted, for he did not say a word that was not verity itself; what she had the pleasure of hearing praised, he had the delight of seeing—to such an extent that their mutual tenderness became more intense by the hour.

On the day when he asked whether she would consent to take him for a husband, she blushed, certainly, but not with alarm; anyone who, seeing her smile, thought that she was toying with the idea of saying no, would have been greatly mistaken.

Unfortunately, the news of the marriage reached the ears of the malevolent Queen, whose sole pleasure was that of troubling the joy of others, and Jacinthe was more detested than anyone else, being more beautiful than all the rest.

꙳ꙮ�꙳

As Jacinthe was strolling in an orchard a short while before the wedding, an old woman approached her, asking for alms, and then suddenly recoiled with a screech, like someone who has almost stepped on a toad.

"Oh, heavens! What have I seen!"

"What's the matter, my good woman, and what have you seen? Speak."

"The ugliest thing on earth!"

"It's surely not me," said Jacinthe, smiling.

"Alas, yes, poor child, it's you. I've been in the world

for a long time, but I've never encountered a person as hideous as you."

"I'm ugly?"

"A hundred times more than one can express."

"What! My eyes . . . ?"

"Are as gray as dust—but that would be nothing if you didn't have the most unpleasant squint."

"My skin . . ."

"One might think that you had rubbed crushed charcoal over your forehead and cheeks."

"My mouth . . ."

"Is as pale as an old autumn flower."

"My teeth . . ."

"If the beauty of teeth were to be broad and yellow, I wouldn't know any more beautiful than yours!"

"Ah! My ears, at least . . ."

"Are so large, red and hairy, under your stringy hair, that one can't look at them without horror. I'm not pretty myself, but I think I'd die of shame if I had ears like yours!"

With that, the old woman—who must have been some wicked fay, a friend of the wicked Queen—fled, uttering a malevolent burst of laughter, while Jacinthe let herself fall, dissolving in tears, on to a bench between two apple trees.

꧁꧂

Nothing was capable of diverting her affliction. "I'm ugly! I'm ugly!" she repeated, incessantly. It was in vain that her fiancé assured her of the contrary, with the most insistent oaths.

"Leave me alone! You're lying, out of compassion. I understand everything now. It's not love you feel for me, it's pity! The beggar-woman had no interest in deceiving me; why would she have done so? It's only too true: I'm ugly. I can't imagine how you can even stand the sight of me."

In order to undeceive her, he thought of bringing many people to her; every man declared that Jacinthe was made exactly as one might wish for the pleasure of the eyes; even a few women said as much, in a somewhat less affirmative fashion. All of that had no effect; the poor child was obstinate in the conviction that she was an object of fright.

"You've made an agreement to make me believe it!"

And when her lover pressed her to fix the date of their marriage regardless, she cried: "Me, your wife? Never! I love you too dearly to make you a gift of something as frightful as me."

You can imagine the despair of that young man, so sincerely smitten. He dropped to his knees, he pleaded, he begged; she always replied in the same way: that she was too ugly to marry.

What could he do? The only means of giving the lie to the old woman, of proving the truth to Jacinthe, would have been to put a mirror before her eyes. But throughout the kingdom there was not a single mirror, and the terror inspired by the Queen was so great that no artisan would have consented to make one.

"Well, I shall go to the court," said the fiancé, finally. "Barbaric as our mistress might be, she can't fail to be moved by my tears and by Jacinthe's beauty. She'll retract, if only for a few hours, the cruel order that does so much harm."

It was not without difficulty that the young woman was persuaded to go to the palace; she did not want to show herself, being so ugly; and then, what use would a mirror be, except to convince her more fully of her irremediable misfortune. However, she ended up consenting, seeing that her friend was weeping.

⁕ᴺᴳᴶᴸ⁕

"What is it?" said the wicked Queen. "Who are these people, and what do they want with me?"

"Majesty, you have before you the most deplorable lover in all the world."

"That's a fine reason for coming to disturb me!"

"Don't be pitiless."

"Eh! What have I to do with your amorous chagrins?"

"If you would permit that a mirror . . ."

The Queen had risen to her feet, quivering with anger. "Someone has dared to mention a mirror!" she said, between her teeth.

"Don't be angry, Majesty, please! And deign to listen to me. This young woman you see before you, so youthful and pretty, has fallen into the strangest error. She imagines that she is ugly . . ."

"Well," said the Queen, with a ferocious laugh, "she's right—for I don't think I've ever seen a more frightful object."

At these words, Jacinthe thought that she would die of sorrow. Doubt was no longer possible, since, in the eyes of the Queen, as in those of the beggar-woman, she was

43

indeed ugly. Slowly, she lowered her eyelids and fell in a faint on the steps of the throne, as if dead.

But the lover, on hearing the cruel remark, did not show such resignation. He cried violently that the Queen was mad, unless she had some reason for lying in that fashion.

He did not have time to add another word; guards had seized him and were holding him solidly; and at a sign from the Queen, a man advanced, who was the executioner; he was always beside the throne, because he might be needed at any moment.

"Do your duty," said the Queen, pointing at the person who had insulted her.

Tranquilly, the executioner raised a large sword, while Jacinthe, not knowing where she was, opened her eyes languidly . . . and two cries rang out, very different from one another: one a cry of joy, because, in the fine steel, Jacinthe had seen herself, so delightfully lovely; and one a cry of anguish, a death-rattle, because the ugly and malevolent Queen had rendered her soul, in the shame and anger of also seeing herself in the improvised mirror.

PRINCESS OISELLE[1]

Although she was very small of stature and could easily have been mistaken for the elder sister of her doll, the daughter of the King of the Golden Isle was the prettiest princess in the world. When he saw that she was of an age to love and be loved, her father asked her whether she felt any repugnance for marriage.

"Oh, no," she said.

"In that case, I'm going to invite to tournaments and balls all the young princes in the region, so that you can make a choice worthy of you and of me."

"Refrain, Father, from inviting so many princes to your court. That will cause you a great deal of expense, needlessly. For a long time I've had a friend by amour, and I'll have nothing more to desire if you give me as a husband the nightingale that sings every evening in the climbing rose outside my window."

The King, as might be imagined, had a great deal of difficulty maintaining the seriousness appropriate to crowned heads. His daughter wanted to marry a bird! He would have a plumaged son-in-law! And it was doubtless in a tree, or in a cage, that the wedding would be held?

---

1. *Oiselle* has a double meaning in French, the literal one referring to a female bird and the familiar one to a silly girl.

These mockeries afflicted the princess cruelly, who went away with a heavy heart; and that evening, leaning on her window-sill while the nightingale sang among the flowers and thorns, she said: "Oh, beautiful bird that I adore, it's no longer time to rejoice, for my father does not want to consent to our espousal."

The nightingale replied: "Don't distress yourself, my Princess. All will be well, since we love one another."

And he consoled her, by singing her the beautiful songs that he knew.

❋⟐❋

At that time, it happened that three giants—they were very famous magicians—came to lay siege to the capital of the realm of the Golden Isle. In order to be redoubtable they had no need to be followed by an army, so robust and cruel were they. They advanced alone all the way to the wall and made it known, by speaking in a tempestuous voice, that if the city was not surrendered to them within three days, they would demolish it stone by stone after having massacred all its inhabitants—and they would not have failed to do what they had said.

The fear was so great that all the mothers ran through the streets, clutching their weeping children to them like marsupials carrying away their little ones. Among the courtiers there were many who wondered whether it would not be wise to submit to the three magicians, for it is more glorious than prudent to remain loyal to the weaker party.

To escape the peril, the King only saw one means: he sent couriers to all the princes in the region, with the mission to announce that he would give his daughter in mar-

46

riage to the man who would deliver him from the giants. But the princes judging the contest unequal, refrained from setting forth on campaign, seductive as the promised recompense was.

In consequence, shortly before nightfall on the third day, everyone was expecting to perish in the rubble of the city, when a few people, watching from the top of the wall, saw the three giants emerge with gestures of pain and fear from the tent where they were taking a nap, and flee like madmen, howling.

The general joy was all the greater because the despair had been so great; however, everyone was lost in conjectures regarding the cause of such an unexpected deliverance.

"Father," said the little princess, "it is the bird I love that it's necessary to thank for this fortunate event. He flew into the tent of your enemies while they were asleep and punctured their eyes with his beak. I think that you should keep your promise and permit me to have for a husband the nightingale of the climbing rose."

But the King, either because he judged the princess's story improbable, or because, in spite of the service rendered, he found the prospect of being the father-in-law of a bird decidedly repugnant, begged his daughter not to pester him any further; he even turned his back on her, in a very bad mood.

That night, while the nightingale was singing his prelude amid the flowers and foliage, she said: "Oh, beautiful bird that I adore, it's no longer time to rejoice, for my father, even though you have delivered him from the giants, does not want to consent to our espousal."

The nightingale replied: "Don't distress yourself, my Princess; all will be well, since we love one another."

And he consoled her by singing her new songs that he had composed.

⁂

Some time afterwards, the palace treasurer disappeared without anyone being able to discover where he had fled, and the great cedar coffer that had previously contained so many rubies, diamonds and pearls was found to be empty.

The King, who was somewhat miserly by nature, was extremely chagrined at having been robbed in that fashion; although he still had many treasures, he never ceased complaining, like a beggar who had been despoiled of all the sous amassed in ten years of "Charity, if you please!" and "May God recompense you!" He had it cried by heralds in all the neighboring realms that he would give his daughter in marriage to the man, prince or not, who could discover the thief and bring back the gems.

That did no good; many days passed and there was no news of the treasurer or the treasure.

One morning, however, as the King was lifting the lid of the coffer sadly, he uttered a cry of joy. All the pearls were there, along with all the rubies and all the diamonds. You might have thought, so brightly was it illuminated, that the room was full of stars.

The King's satisfaction is easily imaginable; however, he would dearly have liked to know who it was that had returned the gems.

"Father," said the princess, "it is to the bird I love that it's necessary to render thanks for this happy event. He had watched and followed the thief; he knew where the treasure was buried. For many days and many nights, with a great deal of difficulty, carrying a ruby in his left foot, a pearl in his right and a diamond in his beak, he traveled from the hiding place to the coffer. I held the window open for him while you were asleep or when you were out hunting. I think you should keep your promise, and permit me to have for a husband the nightingale of the climbing rose.

But the King was no less obstinate than he was miserly. Like many people who are in the wrong, he flew into a temper, and declared to his daughter that he would lock her up in a tower if she ever talked to him again about marriage to such a husband.

That evening, when the nightingale sang his prelude beneath the moonlit branches, she said: "Oh, beautiful bird that I adore, it's no longer time to rejoice, for my father, even though you have returned his treasure to him, does not want to consent to our espousal."

The nightingale replied: "Don't distress yourself, my Princess; all will be well, since we love one another."

And he consoled her by singing her new songs that he had composed for her, which were the sweetest she had ever heard.

※〰〰〰※

The nightingale did not console the princess so effectively that she was not gripped by languor because of her disappointed amour, and she soon died of it. In order to carry her to the royal sepulcher she was put on a bed of white carnations and roses; followed by a tearful crowd, the King marched ahead of the perfumed bier, uttering dolorous cries, which would have moved a heart of marble.

As they arrived at the cemetery, and got ready to lay the pretty corpse in the tomb, a nightingale sang, perched on the branch of a birch tree:

"King, what would you give to the individual who could return to you, alive, the princess for whom you're weeping?"

"To whomever could return her to me," cried the King, "I would give her, I swear, and half my kingdom with her."

"Keep all of your kingdom; your daughter is sufficient for me. But take care not to break your oath."

After saying that, the nightingale came down from the tree, settled on the chin of the dead woman, and with his beak was seen to place a sprig of some herb between her teeth. It was a sprig of the herb that restores life.

The princess was immediately resuscitated.

"Oh, Father," she said, "I think that you ought to keep your promise, finally, and permit me to have for a husband the nightingale of the climbing rose."

Alas, the King had no fear of perjuring himself again. As soon as he had his daughter in his arms, very much alive, he ordered his courtiers to chase the impertinent bird away.

Then something happened that seemed quite astonishing to many people.

The King's little daughter seemed even smaller, and, diminishing further like a snowflake in the sun, she ended up as a small winged creature tinier than an infant's fist. The prettiest of princesses had become the prettiest of little birds. And while her father, repenting too late of his ingratitude, held out his arms desperately, she flew away with the nightingale toward the great woods nearby, where she learned very quickly how to build a nest.

THE ROAD TO PARADISE

AS she had refused to marry the nephew of the Emperor of Germany, the princess had been put, on her father's orders, in the highest chamber of a very high tower—a tower so high that the clouds floated beneath it and even the martins did not come to build their nests there, feeling their wings grow weary before they reached it.

The people who saw from afar the captive's white dress quivering on the platform half way to the heavens believed her to be an angel fallen from paradise rather than a young woman risen from the earth. And all day, and all night too, Guillelmine never ceased to lament, not only because she had been taken away from her companions, with whom she had taken so much pleasure in playing board games or going forth with a falcon on her gauntlet to hunt partridges or herons, but because she was separated from a handsome military page named Aymeri, with blond curls and rosy cheeks, to whom she had given her heart, irrevocably.

For his part, Aymeri was no less desolate at heart, and once, leaning on the window-sill of the cell where he had been imprisoned, looking down at the stony precipice that surrounded the prison, he pronounced these words, sadly:

"What is the point of my being alive, since the one that was the unique joy of my life has been taken away from me? When it was permitted to me to be near her, I took pleasure in hoping for long days full of noble combats and victorious adventures; I desired all glories, which I would have offered to her as a shepherd coming home from the pastures gives his beloved a bouquet of wild flowers; I would have become illustrious in order that she might reward me with a smile. But now that I've been taken away from her, I no longer care about triumphs, or making my name famous throughout the world; what's the point of collecting flowers that won't be kissed by an adored mouth? I can no longer take an interest in anything in this world. You may close, sad eyes that will never see Guillelmine again!"

Having finished speaking, he climbed up on the window -sill, and let himself fall into the stony precipice.

Not long before, however, three swallows had perched not far from there on a branch of a flowering acacia. Flapping their wings and twittering in the stir of the foliage, they had not missed a word of Aymeri's speech, in spite of appearing to pay no heed to it.

"Isn't it a great pity . . ."

"That there is so much chagrin . . ."

"In such a young heart?"

"And that there are so many tears . . ."

"So many bitter tears . . ."

"In such lovely eyes?"

That the birds could speak was not at all surprising, for they were not swallows, in fact, but angels who had taken that form, shrinking their wings. It often happens that celestial spirits mutate in that fashion, in order to listen between the branches or via the chimney to what is being said down below; but they do not do it with any malign intention; they would be quite content only to hear and only to have to repeat honest words. Sometimes, to spare our souls punishment, they even dare to lie to God, who does not hold it against them.

"Don't you think, as I do . . ."

"That it would be just to save Aymeri . . ."

"From such a terrible death?"

"And that, without displeasing the Lord . . ."

"We could carry away that child . . ."

"To our paradise?"

With that, all three of them flew toward the desperate boy at the very moment that he fell from the window, and, before he had collided with the stones of the precipice, they lifted him up toward the heavens on their extended wings, which were now the wings of angels.

Aymeri was quite astonished not to be dead, and was delighted when he knew where he was being taken. He dissolved in thanks, which did not displease his saviors; it is always agreeable, when one obliges someone, not to encounter ingratitude.

Above the houses and palaces, higher than the plane-trees in the gardens and the fir-trees on the hills, the flyers traversed the azure, the light and the clouds. They went so rapidly that the wind, in spite to its desire to follow them, was obliged to give up and stop behind them, out of breath.

Soon, however, when the city had disappeared, down there in the mist, Aymeri was seized by an anxiety.

"Beautiful angels," he asked, "you haven't mistaken the route, have you?"

At these words they could not help laughing.

"Do you think, then, child . . ."

"That we don't know . . ."

"The road to paradise?"

Somewhat ashamed, Aymeri replied: "Forgive me, beautiful angels. I asked you a question that isn't common sense. I promise you that it won't happen again."

The white wings were still beating the air; plains, forests and mountains disappeared into the gray depths. Finally, Aymeri perceived, above the clouds, the summit of a tower.

"Ah!" he said, in a cry of joy. "We've arrived!"

The angels were slightly surprised by those words.

"Not yet! Paradise . . ."

"Isn't as close as you think . . ."

"To somber human dwellings."

"When we have passed . . ."

"To the right of the sun, up there . . ."

"Through flames the color of snow . . ."

"We'll still be far away . . ."

"From the resplendent threshold guarded . . ."

"By cherubim in golden armor."

Aymeri cried, as he clutched at the feathers of the divine messengers: "We've arrived, I tell you! It's on that tower, paradise, on that tower where Guillelmine is raising the sleeves of her dress toward me, more beautiful than your wings!"

The angels were increasingly astonished.

"What, foolish child, you don't want . . ."

"To go with us to the abode . . ."

"Of eternal delights?"

"You don't want, like the elect . . ."

"Who are endlessly ecstatic . . ."

"In light and music . . ."

"To see the incomparable splendor . . ."

"Of miraculous gardens . . ."

"Where flowers that are stars . . ."

"Intoxicate with luminous perfumes . . ."

"And odorous gleams . . ."

"Those celestial bees, souls?"

"You don't want, among the Virgins . . ."

"Lilies more beautiful than lilies . . ."

"Whose marriages make roses . . ."

"To choose a bride . . ."

"Who will strew with imperishable dreams . . ."

"Your angelic nuptial bed?"

But Aymeri, struggling, said:

"No, no! I won't go any further!"

Then the angels drew apart, justly irritated to see that he cared so little for paradisal joys, and through the air, he fell heavily on to the flagstones at the top of the tower.

His limbs broken and his skull fractured, poor Aymeri lay there, blood coming out of his mouth, his eyes and his forehead; he sensed clearly that he was about to die, and throughout his body he experienced pain such as one would never have believed it possible to suffer at that point. But Guillelmine, disheveled, put her arms around his neck, caressing his wounds, kissing his bloody lips. . . .

"I was sure," he said, "that I knew better than they did where the road to paradise was."

GOLDEN KISSES

S HE sang songs that the birds had taught her, but she
sang them better than the birds; he played the tambourine like a dancer from Bohemia, but no gypsy ever
paraded a fingernail so lightly over the taut skin where the
copper plates were clicking; and they traveled the roads
with their music.

Who were they? That question would have embarrassed them greatly. What they remembered was that they
had never slept in a bed or eaten at a table; people who
dwelt in houses or dined before tablecloths were not of
their family; in fact, they had no family at all.

When small, so small that they could barely talk, they
had encountered one another on a road, she emerging
from a bush and he from a ditch—what wicked mothers
had abandoned them?—and immediately they had taken
one another by the hand, laughing. It had rained a little
that day, but in the distance, beneath a gap in the clouds,
the direction was gilded; they had headed toward the sunlight. Since then, they had never had any other itinerary
than going in the direction where the weather was fine.

To be sure, they would have died of thirst and hunger
if streams had not flowed through beds of watercress and
the good women of villages had not thrown them a crust

of bread, too hard for the chickens, from time to time. It was a sad thing to see those vagabond children, so paltry and pale.

One morning, however, when they were already grown up, they were very astonished, on waking up at the foot of a tree, to see that they had been sleeping mouth to mouth. They found that it was good to have joined lips; they continued, with open eyes the kiss of their sleep.

From then on, they no longer cared about their distress; it did not matter to them that they were unfortunate, since they were happy; there is no poverty as cruel as amour is sweet. Scarcely clad in a few rags, through which the sun burned them and the rain soaked them, they did not envy people who wore cool fabrics in summer and fur coats in winter; rags, even with holes in them, are not unpleasant when, beneath those rags, one pleases the person one loves, and more than one great lady would trade her most beautiful dress for the skin of a pretty pauperess.

Going all day from town to town, they stopped in squares outside rich houses whose windows sometimes opened, outside inns where good-humored peasants were at table; she sang her songs and he made his tambourine hum and ring; if they were given a few sous—as happened more than once, for it was pleasant to see and hear them—they were well content; but they were scarcely distressed if no one gave them anything; they only had to go to bed hungry.

It is no great tragedy to have an empty stomach when one has a full heart; starvelings to whom amour offers, beneath the stars, the divine feast of kisses, have nothing of which to complain.

⁂

Once, however, they felt frightfully sad. It was in cold weather, in the north wind, and, having not received any alms for three days, staggering, each of them only finding sufficient strength to sustain the other, they had taken refuge in a barn open to all the winds. They huddled together, hugging one another as tightly as possible, but they still shivered pitiably; even as they kissed, their mouths remembered that they had not had anything to eat.

Oh, the poor things! And with today's despair they had the anxiety of tomorrow. What would they do, what would become of them, if charitable people did not give them any help? Alas, so young, would it be necessary for them to die, abandoned by everyone, on a pile of stones by the roadside, less hard than the human heart?

"What?" she said. "That which all the others have, we shall never have? Is it too much to ask for a little fire at which to warm up, a little bread or an evening meal? It's cruel to think that so many people are sleeping comfortably in good warm houses, and that we're here, trembling with cold, like little birds without feathers and without a nest."

He did not reply; he was weeping.

Suddenly, however, they were able to believe that, dead already, they were in paradise, such a magnificent light there was around them, so radiant did everything seem, and so like an angel was the woman who was advancing toward them in a vermilion brocade dress, with a golden wand in her hand.

"Poor children," she said. "Your misfortune touches me, and I want to come to your aid. After having been poorer than the most wretched, you shall be richer than the most opulent; you shall soon have so many treasures that you will not be able to find enough coffers in all the known lands to contain them."

Hearing that, they thought they were dreaming.

"Oh, Madame, how could such a thing happen?"

"Know that I am a fay, for whom nothing is impossible. Henceforth, every time one of you opens your mouth, a gold coin will emerge, and another, and another, and yet others; it will not take long, therefore, for you to have more wealth than anyone could imagine."

With that, the fay disappeared; and as, because of that prodigy, they remained mute with astonishment, their mouths wide open, so many ducats, sequins, florins, doubloons and other beautiful coins fell from their lips that one might have thought that it was raining gold.

⁂

Some time later, there was rumor in the world of a Duke and Duchess who lived in a palace as large as a city and as dazzling as a starry sky, for the walls, built of the rarest marbles, were encrusted with amethysts and chrysoprases. The splendor of the outside was nothing compared with that was to be seen within. One would never finish if one tried to list all the precious items of furniture, all the golden statues that decorated the rooms, and all the gem-studded chandeliers that scintillated beneath the ceilings. Eyes were blinded by looking at so many marvels. And the masters of the palace held feasts there that everyone agreed in judging incomparable. Tables long enough for an entire people to take their places at them were laden with the most delicate dishes and the most famous wines;

it was on golden platters that the carvers sliced up Tartary pheasants, and into goblets formed from a single fine stone that the wine-waiters poured the wine of the Canary Islands.

If some poor devil who had not eaten since the day before had suddenly come into the dining room, he would have gone mad with astonishment and joy. You can well imagine that there was no lack of guests to admire and praise in every fashion the hosts who treated them so royally. What contributed not a little to put people in a good mood was that the Duke and the Duchess, as soon as they opened their mouths to eat or talk, let fall gold coins therefrom, which the servants collected in baskets and distributed to everyone present after dessert.

The renown of so much wealth and largesse spread so far and wide that it even reached the Land of the Fays. One of them—the one who had appeared in a brocade robe in the barn open to all the winds—formed the project of rendering a visit to her protégés in order to see at close range the happiness that she had given them, and to receive their thanks.

But when she entered, toward nightfall, the sumptuous chamber to which the Duke and Duchess had just retired, she was strangely surprised, for, far from expressing their joy and thanking her, they threw themselves at her feet, their eyes full of tears, sobbing with grief.

"Is it possible," said the fay, "and what do I see? Are you not satisfied with your lot?"

"Alas, Madame, we are so unhappy that we are going to die of chagrin if you don't take pity on us."

"What! You don't think you're rich enough?"

"We're far too rich!"

"Does it displease you only to see gold coins falling from your lips, and, for the sake of a change, would it please you if I made diamonds or sapphires as large as the eggs of turtle-doves emerge?"

"Oh, don't do that!"

"Tell me, then, what afflicts you, because I can't imagine what it is."

"Great Fay, it's very agreeable to warm oneself when one is cold, to sleep in a feather bed, to eat when one is hungry, but there's something even better than all that, and that is to kiss one another on the lips when one is in love. Now, since you have made us rich, we no longer know that happiness, alas, for every time we open our mouths to unite them, detestable sequins emerge, or horrible ducats, and it's the gold that we kiss."

"Ah!" said the fay. "I hadn't thought of that inconvenience. But there's no remedy for that, and you'd do well to get used to it."

"Never! Soften your heart! Can't you retract the frightful present that you've accorded us?"

"Yes, of course—but know that you'll lose not only the gift of spreading gold, but with it, all the riches you've acquired."

"Eh! What does that matter to us?"

"Let it be done then," said the fay, "according to your wish."

And, touched by the wand, they found themselves, in bitterly cold weather, in a barn open to all the winds; what they had been before, they were again: famished, half-naked, shivering with cold like little birds with no feathers and no nest. But they refrained from complaining, and judged themselves exceedingly happy, having their lips on one another's lips.

THE BETROTHAL

When Princess Othilde came into the world people cried out with admiration and astonishment: admiration because she was the prettiest little child imaginable; astonishment because she was no larger than a baby's closed fist. Lying in a cradle no broader than a hand and no longer than a finger, you might have thought her a bird of paradise, without plumage as yet, in her nest. The King and Queen could not weary of admiring her legs and her pink feet, which would have fit into a doll's stockings, her abdomen, like that of a white mouse, and her face, which a daisy-petal would have been sufficient to hide.

To tell the truth, they were worried by seeing her so extraordinarily small, and their royal grandeur could not support the idea of having given birth to a dwarf, but they hoped that their daughter would grow, without losing any of her grace.

They were much mistaken in their expectation; while remaining as gracious as could be, she grew so little that at five years of age she was scarcely taller than a blade of grass, and when playing in the garden pathways she was obliged to stand on tiptoe to pick violets.

Famous physicians were summoned, and promised the richest recompenses if they could succeed in increasing the height of the princess by only a few inches; they conferred with gravity, their hands folded over their chests, blinking behind the lenses of their spectacles, and invented potions that Othilde was obliged to drink, and infallible ointments with which she was rubbed night and morning.

All of that drew a blank; she did not cease to be an adorable dwarf. When she amused herself in the company of her favorite lap-dog, she passed between its legs without having to duck her head.

The King and Queen had recourse to the fays, with whom they had always had an excellent relationship. They did not fail to come, some in litters draped with gold, fringed with precious stones, carried by naked Africans, other in crystal carriages harnessed to four unicorns; there were some who found it more convenient to enter via the window or the chimney, in the form of birds of paradise or martins with blue wings, but as soon as they touched the parquet of the room they became beautiful ladies clad in satin. One after another they touched Othilde with their wands, took her in hand—she was no heavier than a stout skylark—kissed her, blew on her hair, and made signs over her forehead while murmuring omnipotent words.

The charms of the fays had no more effect than the medicines of the savant men. At sixteen, the princess was still so small that, one morning, she was caught in her entirety in a trap set for nightingales in the park

The courtiers, who have an interest in keeping sovereigns joyful, because a good mood ordinarily makes for generosity, did their best to console the King and Queen; they proclaimed that nothing was more ridiculous than tallness, that elevated stature, all things considered, is merely a deformity; as for those who had one, they would dearly have liked to have been half a foot shorter—but it is to royal races that nature reserves such favors!—and when they saw some enormous laborer passing by, they writhed with laughter, holding their sides.

By common accord, the maids of honor, in order that the princess should appear less small beside the shortest of them, renounced wearing the high heels that were fashionable at the time, and the chamberlains adopted the habit of only ever approaching the throne on their knees. But these ingenious flatteries did not always succeed in dispelling the frowns of the King and the Queen; many a time they had a desire to weep when kissing their little girl—with the tips of their lips, for fear of swallowing her—but they held back their tears, in order not to drench her.

As for Othilde, she did not appear to be chagrined by her misfortune; she even had the appearance of taking great pleasure in admiring her pretty little self in a hand-mirror made of a single fairly large diamond.

✢✢✢

However, as all despairs are finally worn away by habituation, the King and the Queen became less sad from day to day. Doubtless they would have ended up no longer being sorry, if something had not happened that was bound to renew their dolor. On the report that had been made of the princess's beauty—for the renown that gladly flatters royal persons had divulged the grace of Othilde everywhere, but not her smallness—the young Emperor of Srinagar fell in love with her and send ambassadors to request her hand in marriage.

You can imagine the embarrassment that such a pro-
posal caused! Of marrying off that little doll, the size of
a parakeet, there could be no question. What man would
accommodate himself to a wife who would surely get lost
at any moment in the nuptial bed?

"Where are you, my beloved?"

"Here, beside you, my love, in a crease in the pillow."

The request of the Emperor of Srinagar was all the
more alarming because his own stature was said to be co-
lossal; he was more handsome than all other princes, but
taller than any giant. On the day of his birth it had been
impossible to find a cradle vast enough for the enormous
prince; it had been necessary to lay him down on long carpets in the throne room. At three years of age he had had
to bend down slightly to take birds from their nests in the
crowns of oak-trees.

His parents, like Othilde's, had consulted physicians
and the fays, just as vainly. He had continued growing, in
an inordinate fashion. When his people, in celebration of
some victory, erected triumphal arches, he was obliged to
dismount from his horse in order to pass through them,
and no matter how high they were, he never failed to bump
the frontons with his helmet, which bore a silver tarasque
with outspread wings.

Naturally, the King and Queen told the ambassadors
that the projected marriage was the most impossible thing
in the world. But the young emperor, very choleric by tem-
perament, was not satisfied with such a response; he did
not want to hear it; the confession of Othilde's small stature seemed to him to be an absurd allegation, imagined
with the intention of ridiculing him, and he shouted as
he put on his helmet, whose silver wings quivered, that

he would put everything to fire and blood to avenge that insult.

⁓ᴗᴗᴗ⁓

He did as he had said. There were terrible battles, cities sacked and entire populations run through by swords—to such an extent the King and Queen saw very clearly what would become of them and the entire country if they did not reach an accommodation with the gigantic conqueror who was marching on the capital, striding over blazing towns and forests. They therefore hastened to request peace, promising no longer to refuse him the hand of their daughter. They were, in any case, fairly tranquil about the consequences of that consent; the emperor, at the sight of Othilde, could not fail to renounce his design and return to his own land with his vainly victorious armies.

Daylight was chosen for the first meeting of the two fiancés, but it took place in the park, not in the palace, because the victor would not have been able to stand upright under the ceilings of the halls.

"Well," he said, "I don't see the princess. Won't she come soon?"

"Look at your feet," said the King.

She was, in fact, there, scarcely taller than the flower-beds to either side of the path; so slim and pretty in her golden dress, her forehead sparkling with gems, she seemed even smaller beside the young and magnificent emperor, whose sunlit armor loomed up against the sky.

"Alas!" he said—for he was desolate on seeing her down there, so charming but so tiny.

"Alas!" she said, in her turn—for she was very sorry to see him, up there, so handsome but so tall.

And they had tears, she in her raised eyes, he in his lowered eyes.

"Sire," said the King, while they were still considering one another from afar, "you can see that you won't be able to marry my daughter. Forced to renounce the honor of your alliance . . ."

But he did not finish his sentence, and, mute with amazement, he looked at the emperor and the princess, she growing and he shrinking, because of the amour, more powerful than the fays, that was attracting them to one another.

Soon they were almost the same height; their lips met, like two roses on the same branch.

THE BAD GUEST

A GREAT anxiety reigned in the court and throughout the kingdom, because the King's son had not taken any nourishment for four days. If he had had a fever or some other malady, no one would have been surprised by that prolonged fast, but the physicians were in accord in saying that the prince, were it not for the great weakness caused by his long abstinence, would have been as well as could be. Why, then, was he depriving himself thus?

There was no other subject of discussion among the courtiers, and even among the commoners; instead of wishing one another "Good day" people accosted one another saying: "Has he eaten anything this morning?" And no one was as anxious as the King himself. That was not because he had a great affection for his son; the young man caused him all kinds of discontentment. Even though he was already sixteen years old, he showed the greatest aversion for politics and the métier of arms; when he attended council meetings he yawned during the finest speeches in a very unbecoming fashion.

Once, charged with going at the head of a small army to punish a gross of rebels, the prince had come back before nightfall, his sword garlanded with convolvulus and his soldiers' arms full of violets and eglantines, giving for a reason that he had found a spring forest on his route, exceedingly pretty to see, and that it is far more amusing to pick flowers than to kill men.

He loved to walk on his own under the trees of the royal park, taking pleasure in listening to the song of nightingales at moonrise. The rare individuals that he allowed to enter his apartments recounted that books were to be seen there scattered on the carpets, and musical instruments—guzlas, psalterions and mandoras—and by night, leaning on his balcony, he spent long hour considering the tiny distant stars in the heavens, his eyes moist with tears.

If you add to all that the fact that he was as pale and frail as a girl, and that instead of putting on chivalric armor, he gladly dressed in bright silken fabrics that reflected the daylight, you will understand that the King was very disappointed to have such a son. But as the young prince was the sole heir to the crown, his salvation was necessary to the wellbeing of the state. So everything imaginable was done, unfailingly, to convince him not to let himself die of hunger.

People pleaded with him, and begged him; he shook his head without responding. They had the most appetizing fish, the most flavorosome meats and the most delicate fruits brought by unparalleled cooks; his table was laid with salmon, trout, pike, haunches of venison, bear's paws, the heads of suckling pigs, hares, pheasants, capercaillies, quail, woodcocks and water-rails at all hours, and the enticing odor of fresh salads rose from twenty dishes. Judging him weary of banal venisons and customary vegetables, he was served fillets of bison, joints of Chinese dogs, minced swifts'-nests, skewered hummingbirds, griblettes of capuchin monkey, brezolles of geuenon, gourmandees of Andean burnets, hacub shoots cooked in antelope fat, marolins from Chandigar and sacramarons from Brazil in a peppered curaçao sauce—but the young prince made a sign that he was not hungry, and after a gesture of ennui, fell back into a reverie.

Things had reached that point, and the King was becoming increasingly desolate, when the child, extenuated, scarcely able to sustain himself, and paler than a lily, spoke to him in these terms:

"Father, if you don't want me to die, give me leave to quit your kingdom and to go wherever seems good to me, without being followed by anyone."

"Eh! Weak as you are, you'd faint before taking three steps, my son."

"It's in order to recover strength that I want to go away. Have you read what is recounted of Thibaut the Rhymer,[1] the troubadour who was the captive of the fays?"

"It's not my custom to read," said the King.

"Know, then, that in the land of the fays, Thibaut led a very happy life, and was content at meal times most of all, because little pages, who were gnomes, served him for soup a drop of dew on an acacia leaf, for roast meat a butterfly wing gilded by a ray of sunlight, and for dessert, what remains on a rose petal of the kiss of a bee."

"A meager dinner!" said the King, who could not help laughing in spite of his anxieties.

"It is, however, the only one I desire. I can't nourish myself, like other men, on the flesh of slain beasts, nor vegetables born of mud. Let me go to the land of the fays,

---

1. Mendès improvised this Provençal equivalent of Thomas the Rhymer, the protagonist of a popular Scottish ballad whose fame was greatly extended by Walter Scott, but he refers to the model by name in another tale in the present collection.

and if they invite me to their feast, I'll eat in accordance with my hunger and return full of health."

What would you have done, in the King's place? Since the young prince was on the point of dying, it was a kind of wisdom to consent to his folly; his father therefore let him depart, not hopeful of seeing him again.

As the realm was near the forest of Broceliande, the child did not have very far to go to reach the land of the fays. They gave him a very good welcome, not because he was the son of a powerful monarch, but because he liked listening to the song of nightingales at moonrise and leaning on his balcony gazing at the distant stars. A feast was held in his honor in a vast hall with walls of pink marble, illuminated by diamond chandeliers; the most beautiful of the fays, for the pleasure of his eyes, danced in a circle, holding hands, allowing their scarves to trail.

He experienced a joy so great, in spite of the cruel pangs of his stomach, that he would have liked the dances to last forever. However, he was becoming weaker and weaker, and he understood that it would not be long before he died if he did not take some nourishment. He confessed to one of the fays that state he was in, and even dared to ask what time they ate supper.

"Oh, whenever you like," she said.

She gave an order, and then a page, who was a gnome, brought the prince, for soup, a drop of dew on an acacia leaf. Oh, what excellent soup! The fays' guest declared that it was impossible to imagine better. Then he was offered for a roast a butterfly wing gilded by a ray of sunlight—a hawthorn spike served as a skewer—and he ate it in a single mouthful, delightedly. But what charmed him most of all was the dessert, the trace of a bee's kiss on a rose-petal.

"Well, my child," said the fay, "have you supped well?"

He made an affirmative gesture—ecstatic, even—but at the same time he lowered his head and died of starvation.

That was because he was one of those poor individuals —like the poets down here—who are both too pure and not pure enough, too divine to share the feasts of humans, but too human to sup with the fays.

THE MONEY-BOX

JOCELYNE was a beggar-girl on a road where no one passed by—with the consequence that no money ever fell into the frail hand, weary of being held out. Sometimes, from a branch shaken by the wind, a flower shed a petal in the direction of the pauperess, and a rapidly-flying swallow gave her alms, in a flutter of wings, of a shrill cry, but they were chimerical offerings that one cannot offer in payment to the miserly individuals who sell things to eat or things in which to clothe oneself, and Jocelyne had a good deal to complain about—all the more so because, born she knew not when of she knew not whom, having no other memory than that of having woken up, one morning when the sun was shining, under a bush by the roadside, she did not go home at night to one of those fine cottages full of the odor of soup, where other little girls, after having offered their foreheads to their mother and father, went to sleep in warm straw, on the bread-bin, in front of a fire of vine-branches, which also went to sleep.

She resigned herself to climbing, as soon as night fell, into an elm or an oak, and sleeping stretched out along a stout branch, not far from squirrels, which, knowing her well and not being afraid of her, leapt on to her arm, her

73

shoulder or her head, playing with their little paws in her bushy hair, the color of gold and so bright that it was as difficult to fall asleep in the tree as in a room where there was a light. When the nights were cold, she would gladly have curled up in some oriole's or blackbird's nest, if she had not been too big.

Her clothing was made of an old canvas sack, found one lucky day in a roadside ditch; she patched it with green leaves every spring. As she was youthful and pretty, with florid cheeks, you might have taken that garment for the foliage of a rose. As for her nourishment, she scarcely knew any other than the cob-nuts of the wood and the sorb-apples of the pathways; her great feast was to eat grasshoppers grilled on a thorn over a little fire of dried grass.

You can easily see that Jocelyne was the most wretched creature imaginable, and if her lot was already cruel enough during the good season that puts warmth in the air and fruits on the bushes, think what it must have been like when the north wind sacked the sterile hazelnut-trees and froze the skin through her rags of dead leaves.

Once, when she was coming back from collecting cob-nuts, she saw a fay clad in golden muslin emerging from the greenery of a thorn-bush. The fay spoke, in a voice softer than the sweetest music.

"Jocelyne, because you have a heart as kind as your face is charming, I want to make you a gift. You see this tiny money-box, which has the form and color of a carnation bud? It belongs to you. Don't fail to put everything precious that you possess into it; on the day when you break it, it will render what it has received a hundredfold."

With that, the fay vanished like a flame snuffed out by a gust of wind, and Jocelyne, who had conceived some hope when the lady appeared, felt sadder than ever. That could not be a good fay! Was there anything more cruel than to give a money-box to a poor girl who had neither a sou nor a farthing? What could she, who possessed nothing, put into it? The only savings she had were her memories of days without bread, and sleepless nights in the icy wind and snow. She was tempted to break that present against the stones, because it was a mockery for her, but she dared not, finding it pretty; and, full of melancholy, she wept.

The tears fell, one by one, into the money-box no larger than a flower, like a blossoming carnation.

⁂

Another time, she had a stroke of luck that rendered her even more unhappy. On the road along which no one passed, the King's son, returning from a hunt, went by, a hawk on his wrist. Mounted on a horse that was shaking its snowy mane, clad in blue satin with a silver flower-pattern, his face proud, and so luminous in the sunlight that one would not have been astonished to see the red flower of is lips bloom, the prince was so handsome that the beggar-girl thought she was seeing an archangel in a nobleman's costume. Her eyes wide, her mouth open, she held out her hand toward him, and she felt something, which must have been her heart, emerge from within her and follow him!

Alas, he drew away, without even having seen her. Alone, as before—more alone, for having momentarily ceased to be—she allowed herself to fall on to the far side of the ditch, closing her eyes, doubtless in order that nothing should replace the adorable vision.

When she opened them again, she perceived the money -box beside her, which bore a slight resemblance to parted lips. She seized it, and with the desperate impulsiveness of her vain amour, putting her soul into her breath, she kissed it, with a long kiss. But the fay's present, under that ardent caress, was no more moved than a stone.

And from that day on, Jocelyne knew such dolors that nothing she had endured until then could compare with them; she remembered, as glorious hours, the times when she had only suffered from hunger and cold; going to sleep half-starving, shivering in the squalls, was nothing, or very little, now that she was no longer ignorant of veritable anguish.

She thought that other women, at court, illustrious and ornamented—"not as pretty as you," said the mirror of the spring—could see the handsome prince with the luminous visage at almost any time; that he approached them, that he talked to them, that he smiled at them. Before long, no doubt, some glorious young woman, come from Trebizond in a litter borne by a white elephant with a gilded trunk, would marry the King's son. She, however, the beggar-girl of the road devoid of passers-by, would continue to live—since it is living to die a little every day— in that solitude, in that misery, far from the man she loved so tenderly. She would never see him again—never, never! On the night of the royal wedding she would be sleeping in her tree, on a branch, not far from the squirrels; and while the spouses were embracing one another amorously, she would be biting the hard bark of the oak with rage.

Rage? No. Dolorous as she was, she had no anger; her greatest chagrin was thinking that the son of the King might perhaps not be loved by the princess of Trebizond as much as he was by her, a poor girl.

⁂

Finally, one day when it was snowing, she resolved not to suffer any more. She no longer had the strength to support so many torments. She decided to throw herself into the lake in the middle of the forest. She would scarcely feel the chill of the water, being accustomed to the chill of the air.

Shivering, she set forth, walking as quickly as she could. It was a gray morning, under the weight of snowflakes. Amid the sadness of the white ground, leafless trees, bristling bushes and dismal horizons, nothing was shining but her golden hair; one might have thought it a little of the sun, remained behind. She walked even more rapidly.

When she arrived on the shore of the lake, because of the snow, she had a wedding-dress over her rags.

"Adieu!" she said.

Adieu? Yes, to him alone.

And she was about to let herself fall into the water when the fay, in a robe of golden muslin, emerged from between the branches of a thorn-bush.

"Jocelyne," she said, "why do you want to die?"

"Don't you know, wicked fay, how unhappy I am? The most frightful death would be sweeter to me than life."

The fay laughed, softly.

"Before drowning yourself," she said, "you ought at least to break the money-box."

77

"What's the point of that, since, being so poor, I haven't put anything into it?"

"Well, break it anyway," said the fay.

Jocelyne dared not disobey; having taken the futile present from beneath her rags, she broke it on a stone.

Then, while the wintry forest became a magnificent palace of porphyry with azure ceilings starred with gold, the handsome son of the King emerged from the shattered money-box, took the beggar-girl in his arms, and kissed her hair, her forehead and her lips a hundred times. At the same time he asked her whether she would accept him as a husband.

And Jocelyne wept with joy, and carried on weeping. The good money-box returned her the tears of sadness a hundredfold, just as it had rendered her the kiss, in tears of happiness.

THE GOOD RECOMPENSE

NOTHING could distract the chagrin of Princess Modeste, and you would have felt pity for her if you had been able to see her. Not that she had become ugly by dint of weeping—when one is as pretty as she was, one does not cease to be so—but she got paler every day; she was a pink rose changed into a white rose.

In vain her maids of honor did their best to relieve her worries; she did not deign to smile at their songs or their dances. If, at meal-times, she was offered pearl jam, of which she had previously been very fond, she turned her head away with a sigh. She reached the point of pushing her favorite pet monkey away with her foot, which was poor payment for its capers. Saddened by the joy of others, she had the door to the cage of her parakeets opened, whose chatter was importunate. She did not even take pleasure any longer in looking at herself in the mirror while her maidservants put flowers and precious stones in her hair.

In sum, it would be impossible to imagine a desolation like that of Princess Modeste, and hearts of stone would have melted.

I shall leave you to imagine how anxious the King must have been, who loved his daughter dearly. He had no appetite for anything, no longer interested himself in affairs of State and yawned at the flatteries of his courtiers —to the point that one day, he watched the hanging of two ministers without the slightest satisfaction, although spectacles of that sort had always had the privilege of putting him in a good mood.

What upset him most of all was that the princess was obstinate in not revealing the cause of her chagrin; he lost hope of curing a dolor of which he did not know the cause.

"Tell me, my daughter," he said, "is there something you lack?"

"Hic, hic!" replied the princess, in tears.

"Would you like a dress the color of stars or the dawn?"

"Hic, hic!"

"Would you like me to summon guitar players of renowned ballad singers to chase away your melancholy?"

"Hic, hic!"

"Has it come to your mind that it would be pleasant to be married to the handsome son of some king perceived at a tournament?"

"Hic, hic!"

No other response could be obtained. Once, however, by dint of being begged, the princess ended up admitting that if she was grief-stricken in that fashion, it was because she had lost something.

"Well, my daughter, why didn't you say so sooner. Whatever you've lost will be found. What is that precious object, if you please?"

But at that question, Modeste uttered a frightful cry, and hid her head in her hands, like someone who is ashamed.

"Never," she stammered, "never will I name the object I regret. Only know that it was a gift of the fays, in muslin, that it was the most beautiful in the world, with its embroideries and its gold lace, as light and luminous as a morning cloud, that it must have been stolen from me one summer day when I was bathing with my ladies-in-waiting in the stream under the willows, and that I shall surely die if I don't get it back."

With that, blushing deeply, she fled to her apartment, and the good father's heart was wrung on hearing her plaints and fits of sobbing through the door.

Although the information given by Modeste was not very precise, and the description of the item lost or stolen was not of a nature to avoid confusions, the King resolved to put to work the only means he had of consoling his daughter's despair. Couriers ran around the entire city, and were sent to the smallest villages in the most remote areas, with the mission of announcing that the princess, while frolicking near the stream, under the willows, had lost a very precious object, the most beautiful in the world, in muslin, ornamented with fine embroidery and gold lace as light and luminous as a morning cloud. With regard to the recompense for whoever brought it back, the King let it be known that he would not recoil before any sacrifice, that he engaged himself by a solemn oath to refuse nothing that was asked of him.

Needless to say, that proclamation put the entire country astir. People who had made any discovery, far from the river, devoid of lace or embroidery, nevertheless dreamed beautiful dreams, and those who had not found anything at all set about searching dutifully.

There was a great crowd under the willows from dawn to dusk and all along the watercourse: men, women and children bending over the grass, parting the branches, breathless with hope, imagining that at any moment they were about the put their hand on their fortune; and for an entire week, a thousand vain trivia were brought to the palace—coins, strips of ribbon, turn gloves—that bore no resemblance to the description given by the couriers.

Every time that someone presented a new object, the princess turned her head away, made a negative gesture, and plunged more profoundly into her melancholy.

Now, it happened one day that a young fisherman, very shapely in his person and very agreeable to look at in spite of his coarse rags, came into the courtyard of the palace and said, confidently, that he wanted to speak to the King. The first thought the halberdiers had was to throw the wretch out; one does not converse with crowned individuals when one has nothing on one's head but a paltry red woolen bonnet discolored by the wind and rain. But as soon as the fisherman had affirmed in a loud voice that he had something in his coat pocket that would bring the smile back to the lips of the princess, the guards adopted a much less forbidding attitude, and the young man was introduced into the throne room.

On seeing him, the King shrugged his shoulders.

"Evidently," he said, "this one will be no more fortunate than the others; my daughter, once again, will not have the contentment for which she hopes."

"Sire," said the fisherman, "Your Majesty is mistaken. Thanks to me, Princess Modeste will get out of difficulty."

"Is that possible?"

"It's certain."

At the same time, the young fisherman, who would have been as handsome as the son of an emperor had he been clad in velvet or brocade, took out from his coat something light and long, wrapped in pink paper.

"Within this paper," he said, "is the object lost by the princess, and I think she will agree with that, if Your Majesty cares to send it to her."

"I consent to that."

At a sign from His Majesty, a chamberlain, having taken the pink parcel, went to take it to the princess.

To tell the truth, the tranquility of the fisherman and the firm tone in which he spoke had inspired some confidence in Modeste's father. It might be the case that the young man had found the gift of the fays . . . but no, it was a vain hope, a chimera—Modeste would be as sad today as she was every other day.

A burst of laughter sang out, lively, bright and joyful, like a tinkle of breaking glass, and the princess, pink with pleasure, running as if she were dancing, raced into the hall and threw her arms around her father's neck.

"Oh, what happiness! I have it! I have it! How glad I am! Oh, my good father! Also, see, I'm laughing like a madwoman—me, who never ceased weeping!"

It would be difficult to express the satisfaction of the King on hearing these words. In spite of etiquette, he started laughing himself, and as the courtiers did not fail to imitate him, and as the valets in the antechambers and the halberdiers at the gate, hearing everyone laughing, thought that they ought to laugh too, there was such a joyful tumult of hilarity throughout the palace that the princess's pet monkey, standing on the train of her dress, could not hold back, and held his sides, spluttering.

Meanwhile, the King turned to the man to who that happy event was owed.

"I have given my royal word, and will not break it. Whatever you desire, speak without dread; I shall grant it to you."

The young fisherman knelt down. "Sire, I could request of you riches, positions and titles; because of your oath, you would not fail to make me rich, powerful and glorious. But I have no such aims. Since I have brought back to the princess the object that disappeared while she was bathing with her ladies-in-waiting under the willows by the stream, I only ask that I be given—the lining!"

"The lining!" cried the King, full of astonishment. "Is it, then, a robe or a mantle that my daughter was mourning?"

"Perhaps, sire. Whatever it is, I'm asking for is it . . ."

"Lining. I heard you. And I promise that you shall have it. For, after all, your discretion is praiseworthy. When it would be permissible for you to request all treasures and all honors, you limit yourself . . ."

But that sentence remained incomplete; the princess blushing to the roots of her hair, fell in a faint on the steps of the throne. For what she had lost and recovered was her chemise; the fisherman was asking for a strange recompense.

In any case, the King could not refuse, since his word had been given, to marry his daughter to the subtle young man; and when the day of the wedding came, seeing the groom more handsome than any prince in his garments of brocade and velvet, Modeste thought, without overmuch fear, about what would become of the exceedingly precious gift of the fairies, ornamented with embroideries and gold lace as diaphanous as a morning cloud.

THE LOST WORDS

IT happened once that a very cruel fay, as pretty as the flowers and as nasty as the serpents that hide beneath them, resolved to avenge herself on the entire people of a great country.

Where was that country situated? In the mountains or in the plain, on the banks of a river or the shore of the sea? The story does not say. Perhaps it neighbored a realm where the couturiers are skilled in embroidering moons and stars on the robes of princesses. And to what offense had the fay been subjected? The story does not say that either. Perhaps she had not been invited to the baptism of the King's daughter. Whatever opinion it pleases you to have on those two matters, be assured that she was very angry.

She wondered first of all whether, in order to desolate the country, she ought not to have the thousand little genii that served as her pages set fire to all the palaces and all the cottages, whether she ought not to wither all the lilies and all the roses therein, and whether she ought not to render all the young women as ugly as old and toothless crones. She would have been able to unleash tarasques in the streets, vomiting smoke and flames, or to order the sun to make a detour in order not to pass over the detested city, to command storms to uproot the trees and knock down the buildings—but she settled on a design even more abominable.

As a thief who is not pressed for time chooses the most precious jewels from a casket, she took away from the memory of men and women the three divine words: "I love you"—and slipped away, the evil deed done, with a little snigger that would have been more frightful than the devil's laughter if she had not had the rosiest lips in the world.

⁂

In the beginning, the women and men only half-perceived the injury that had been done to them. It seemed to them that they were lacking something, but they did not know what. Fiancés who arranged to meet at dusk in arbors of rose-bushes, spouses who spoke to one another in low voices at casements, thinking of the imminent delights that would arive after the windows were shuttered and the curtains drawn, interrupted themselves abruptly while gazing at one another or kissing one another; they sensed that they wanted to say something to which they were accustomed, but they did not have the slightest idea what that phrase had been; they remained astonished and anxious, not questioning one another, because they did not know what question to ask, so complete had been the forgetfulness of the precious words; but they did not suffer too much yet, having the consolation of so many other murmured words, and so many caresses.

Alas, they did not take long to be gripped by a profound melancholy. It was in vain that they adored one another, that they called one another by the most tender names,

that they made the sweetest proposals; it was not sufficient for them to proclaim that all delights blossom in the
rose of a kiss, to swear that they were ready to die, him for
her and her for him, to call one another "my soul," "my
passion" or "my dream." They had an instinctive need to
proffer and hear another word, more exquisite than all
words, and, with the bitter memory of the ecstasies that
were within it came the anguish of never again being able
to pronounce or hear it.

After the sadness, there were the quarrels. Judging their
happiness incomplete, because of the confession henceforth forbidden to the most ardent lips, lovers demanded
of one another—without saying why, being unable to say
why—the one thing that neither of them could give. They
accused one another mutually of coldness or treachery,
not believing in tenderness that was not expressed as they
would have wished—with the consequence that soon fiancés ceased to arrange rendezvous amid the flowering
rose-bushes, and even after the windows were shuttered,
conjugal bedrooms no longer heard any but cold conversations in armchairs that did not draw together.

Can there be any joy where there is no love? Ruined by
wars, devastated by plagues, the country that the fay hated
would not have been as desolate and as bleak as it had
become because of the three forgotten words.

⁂

There was in that unfortunate country a poet who had a
great deal to mourn. It was not that, having some beautiful mistress, he despaired of no longer being able to say
or hear the stolen words; he had no mistress, being too

fond of verses. It was because it was impossible for him to conclude a poem begun the day before the malevolent fay had accomplished her vengeance. And why? Because the poem, rightly, had to conclude with "I love you," and could not possibly finish in any other fashion.

The poet struck his forehead, took his head in his hands, and asked himself: "Am I going mad?" He was, however, certain that he had found, before undertaking his ode, the words that preceded that final exclamation mark. The proof that he had found these words was that the line with which they were to rhyme, already written, awaited them, required them, and did not want any others, like a mouth that, in order to become a kiss, awaits a twin mouth. But the indispensable, fatal phrase, he had forgotten, and could not even remember ever having known it.

Certainly, there was some mystery there, and that was enough to cause the poet to dream incessantly, with a bitter melancholy—oh, the sadness of interrupted poems!—on the edges of woods, near clear springs, where it is the custom of fays to come to dance in circles in the evenings, by starlight.

⁂

Once, when he was dreaming under the branches, the malevolent thieving fay perceived him, and fell in love with him. A fay is not the kind of person to be inhibited by anything; more rapidly than a butterfly kisses a rose, she put her lips to his—and the poet, occupied as he was with his ode, nevertheless found that caress exquisite.

In the profundities of the earth, grottoes of blue and pink diamonds opened, and gardens bloomed of lilies as luminous as stars; it was there that a golden chariot harnessed to winged moles, which cleaved the earth as they flew, carried the poet and the fay, and for a long time they loved one another there, forgetful of everything that was not their kisses or their smiles.

If they ceased momentarily to have their mouths united or to gaze into one another's eyes, it was to take pleasure in the most delightful diversions: gnomes clad in zinzolin satin, and formosas[1] dressed in the mist of lakes, performed dances before them to the music of invisible orchestras, while flying hands that had no arms presented them with ruby baskets of snowy fruits, perfumed like white roses and a virgin's breast; or, in order to please her, he recited to her, while plucking the strings of a theorb, the most beautiful verses imaginable.

Fay as she was, she had never known a joy comparable to that if having that handsome young man sing to her, who invented new odes every day, and she sensed that she might die of tenderness when she felt, after he fell silent, the breath of a very close mouth running through her hair.

And there were, after many days of happiness, more days of happiness, incessantly. However, she sometimes had morose reveries, her cheek in her hand, her hair falling in golden streams all the way to her hips.

"What is saddening you, then, O Queen? What more can you desire, in the midst of our pleasures, you who are omnipotent, you who are beautiful?"

---

1. I have given the usual English equivalent of the authors' *"formoses,"* although I cannot find any other instance of the word being employed in the context implied here. The Latin *formosus*, however, means beautiful, and Mendès is undoubtedly deriving the term therefrom, perhaps idiosyncratically.

She did not reply at first; but when he insisted, she sighed: "Alas, one ends up suffering for the evil one has done. Alas, I am sad because you have never said to me: 'I love you.'"

He did not pronounce the phrase, but he uttered a cry of joy, at having rediscovered the end of his poem.

The fay tried in vain to retain him in the grotto of blue and pink diamonds, in the gardens of lilies as luminous as stars; he returned to the earth, finished, wrote and published the ode, in which the men and women of the sad country rediscovered in their turn the divine lost words.

In consequence, there were, as before, rendezvous in the bushes, and tender conversations at conjugal windows.

It is because of verses that kisses are sweet, and lovers do not say anything that poets have not sung.

THE HEART'S MEMORY

THE kingdom was in desolation because the young king, since he had become a widower, no longer occupied himself with affairs of State, spending days and nights weeping before a portrait of the dear departed.

That portrait, he had made himself once, having learned to paint with that express purpose; for there is nothing crueler for a lover or a truly smitten spouse than to leave to someone else the care of reproducing the beauty of the beloved; artists have a fashion of looking closely at their models that cannot please a jealous man; they do not put on the canvas all that they have seen; something must remain in their eyes, and in their hearts too.

And that portrait, now, was the young king's only consolation; he could not hold back his tears when he gazed at it, but he would not have exchanged the bitterness of those tears for the sweetness of the happiest smiles.

It was in vain that his ministers came to him to say: "Sire, we have received disquieting news; the new King of Ormuz is raising a vast army to invade your estates." He pretended not to hear them, his gaze still fixed on the adored image.

One day, he flew into a range and nearly killed one of his chamberlains, the latter having ventured to insinuate that the most legitimate grief ought not to be eternal, that his master would do well to think about marrying some young woman—the niece of an emperor or the daughter of a peasant, it did not matter.

"Monster!" cried the inconsolable widower. "Do you dare to give me such craven advice? You want me to be unfaithful to the most lovable of queens? Remove yourself from my sight, or you'll perish by my own hand. But before leaving, know, in order to repeat it to everyone, that no woman will ever sit on my throne or sleep in my bed, unless she is exactly similar to the one I have lost!"

He knew that in speaking thus he was scarcely making any engagement. Such as she was revived in her golden frame—but dead, alas!—the queen was so perfectly beautiful that one would not have found her peer anywhere on earth. Brunette, with long, supple hair that flowed like liquid ebony, a slightly elevated forehead, of amber-tinted ivory, profound eyes as dark as night, her mouth opened by a smile in which all her teeth were shining, she defied comparisons and resemblances, and even a princess who had received in her cradle the most precious gifts of all the good fays could not have had such beautiful dark hair, such profound dark eyes, nor that forehead, nor that mouth.

⚜

Many months went by—more than a year—without bringing any fortunate change in the sad state of things. Increasingly alarming news was received from Ormuz; the King did not deign to pay any heed to the growing danger. It is true that the ministers levied taxes in his name, but as they kept the money instead of employing it to equip soldiers, the country could not fail to be ravaged, after having paid not to be. In consequence, there were groups of people outside the palace every day, who came to plead and to complain.

The dead woman's lover did not emerge from his melancholy; his only attention was for the silent charm of the portrait. Once, however—it was at the hour when dawn tints windows pink and blue—he turned to the casement, listening to a song that was fading away: a faint and high-pitched song as pretty and matinal as the lilt of a skylark. He took a few steps, astonished, stuck his forehead to the window and looked out.

He could scarcely retain a cry of pleasure. He had never seen anything as charming as that young shepherdess leading her flock of sheep to the meadows. She was blonde to the point that her hair gilded the sun rather than being gilded by it. She had a slightly low forehead, as pink as young roses, bright eyes with an auroral clarity, and her laughing mouth as so narrow that, even opened by the song, it scarcely allowed a glimpse of five or six little pearls.

But the king, charmed as he was, fled from that spectacle, putting his hands over his closed eyelids, and, ashamed at having been deflected momentarily from the defunct beauty, returned to the portrait, knelt down, weeping with dolor and delight; he no longer remembered that a shepherdess had passed beneath his window, singing.

"Oh, you are quite sure," he groaned, "that my mourning heart will belong to you forever, since no other woman exists who resembles you; and it would be necessary, for me to make a queen, in order that in a mirror in which she would be eternalized, your living image would emerge!"

The following day, while admiring the portrait of the dead woman, he had a painful surprise. He thought, and said to himself: *That's very strange. This room must be damp; the air one breathes here isn't good for paintings. For, in sum, I remember perfectly that my queen's hair was not as dark as I see it. No, certainly, it did not have that darkness of liquid ebony. It was sunlit here and there, I remember that—the color of dawn, not of dusk.*

He asked for his brushes and his palette, and quickly corrected the portrait that the damp air had spoiled.

Good! That's definitely the golden hair that I loved so recklessly, that I shall always love.

And, full of a bitter joy, on his knees before the image now similar to its cherished model, he renewed his oaths of eternal constancy.

Truly, however, some malevolent genius had to be toying with him. Three days having gone by, he was obliged to recognize that the portrait had once again suffered notable deterioration. What did it mean? Why was that ivory forehead, tinted with amber, so high? He had a good memory, thank God! He was sure that the queen had had a small forehead, as pink and fresh as young eglantines.

With a few strokes of the brush, he lowered the gilded hairline and tinted the forehead pink, brightly. And he felt his heart full of an infinite tenderness for the restored portrait.

The following day, it was even worse. It was evident that the eyes and mouth of the portrait had been changed by some accident, or a mysterious will. The beloved had never had those dark eyes, as dark as night, nor that excessively open mouth, which showed almost all the teeth. Oh, entirely to the contrary, the matinal blue of the sky, where skylarks trilled, did not equal in softness the azure of the eyes with which she gazed at her beloved; and as for her mouth, it was so narrow that, even open for a song or a kiss, it scarcely allowed a glimpse of a few dainty pearls.

The young king felt himself gripped by a violent anger against that absurd portrait, which contradicted so many cherished memories. If he had had in his power the execrable enchanter to whom that transformation was due— for there was surely some enchantment in it—he would have avenged himself on that man in a terrible fashion. It would not have taken much for him to take down the lying image and trample it underfoot. He calmed down, though, thinking that the damage was reparable.

He set to work; he painted in accordance with his faithful memories, and a few hours later, there was on the canvas a young woman with eyes as blue as the distance of the dawn, and a mouth so small that, if it had been a flower, it would scarcely have been able to contain two or three drops of dew. And he gazed at his queen, full of a dolorous delight.

"That's her! Oh, that's really her!" he sighed.

As a result, he had no objection to make on the day when the chamberlain, who had the custom of peeping through keyholes, advised him to take for a wife a lovely shepherdess who went by outside the palace every morning, singing a song, because she resembled in every detail—although perhaps she was slightly prettier—the portrait of the beautiful queen.

THE THREE GOOD FAYS

IN those days there were three fays, named Abonde,
Myrtile and Caricine, who were good to an extent that
one can hardly conceive. They only took pleasure in coming to the aid of the unfortunate, and that was how they
employed all their power. Nothing could persuade them
to join in the games of their peers on moonlit nights in
the forest of Broceliande, or to sit down at feasts at which
cup-bearing sylphs poured drops of dew into the calices
of lilies—according to Thomas the Rhymer, there is no
beverage more agreeable—if they had not consoled many
human dolors first; and they had hearing so keen that they
could hear, even from far away, hearts contracting and
tears flowing.

Abonde, who visited for preference the outlying districts of large cities, would suddenly appear in poor dwellings, either breaking a window-pane—which was quickly
replaced by a pane of diamond without there being any
need to call a glazer—or by entering into the substance of
the smoke of a dying stove; seized by pity at the sight of
mansards in which wretched families devoid of work were
shivering and dying of hunger, she had soon transformed
them into sumptuous dwellings, well-equipped with fine
furniture, a larder full of food and coffers full of gold coins.

No less charitable, Myrtile mainly frequented rural folk, who lament in their thatched cottages when the hail has ruined the flowering promise of the orchards, and who, between the bin devoid of bread and the cupboard devoid of linen, wonder if it might not be wiser to abandon their children in the wood, having no means to nourish or dress them. She easily succeeded in rendering them courage, offering them talismans, advising them to make wishes that never failed to come true, so that those who, three minutes earlier, would not have been able to offer crumbs to a robin tapping in the window with its beak, found themselves well-to-do in fully-provisioned houses, or powerful monarchs in palaces of porphyry and precious stones.

As for Caricine, it was the chagrins of lovers that moved her more than any other difficulty; she rendered coquettes and the inconstant faithful, softened the hearts of miserly parents who refused to consent to their children's happiness, and when she learned that a young vagabond beggar was smitten with the daughter of a king, she metamorphosed him into a prince as handsome as the day, in order that he could marry his beloved.

In consequence, if things had gone on like that for any length of time there would have been no more poverty or chagrin in the world, thanks to the three good fays.

That would not have been to the liking of a very cruel enchanter, who was animated by the most evil sentiments with regard to men and women; the mere idea that people would cease to suffer and weep on earth caused him unbearable torment. He therefore felt full of wrath against those excellent fays, not knowing which of the three he detested the most, and he resolved to render them incapable of bringing, as was their custom, succor to the unfortunate. Nothing was easier for him, because of the great power that he had.

He summoned them to appear before him; then, frowning, he announced that they would be deprived, for many centuries, of their magical power, adding that he intended to transform them into vile malign beasts or mindless objects such as blocks of marble, tree-trunks or woodland streams, but that he deigned, out of mercy, to permit them to chose the forms in which they would spend their time of penitence.

It is impossible to form any idea of the chagrin that the good fays experienced. It was not that they were inordinately sad about losing their glory and their privileges; it cost them little to renounce dances in the forest of Broceliande and feasts in subterranean palaces illuminated by ruby suns; what broke their hearts was that, once having fallen, they would no longer be able to help the wretched.

What! thought Abonde. *Men and women are going to die of cold and hunger in suburban mansards and I'll no longer be able to console them!*

Myrtile said to herself: *What will become of the peasants in their thatched cottages when downpours of hail have broken the branches of the flowering apple-trees? How many little children will weep, abandoned in the pathless undergrowth, perceiving no light, while the wolves lie in wait for them, but the distant lamp lit by the wife of the ogre?*

And Caricine, while sobbing, thought: *How many lovers will suffer! I've just been informed of a poor little street singer, without a house or family, languishing of tenderness for the Princess of Trebizond. He won't marry her, then, alas?*

And all three of the good fays were in distress for a long time, as if they were suffering all the dolors with they would not be able to turn into joys, and shedding all the tears that they would not be able to wipe away.

To tell the truth, they had, in their despair, one small consolation. It was permitted to them to design the appearances under which they would live among humans; their generosity, thanks to a fortunate choice, might perhaps still find a means of exercise. Although reduced to the impotence of moral individuals or perishable things, they would not be entirely useless to poor humans. They started to reflect, therefore, wondering what it might be useful to be, in order not to cease being helpful.

Abonde, who recalled the poverty of the outlying districts, initially conceived the desire to be mutated into a rich person, who could distribute alms without counting them. Then again, thinking about extinct stoves and beds without covers, she would not have been displeased to become a warming flame or a good bed in which weary laborers could repose.

Myrtile dreamed of being a queen who would make liveried chamberlains of all the laborers dressed in rags, or a sunbeam that parts dark clouds, or a woodcutter's wife who brings lost children back home.

As for Caricine, with her design of being kind to hearts, she would gladly have consented to be turned into a beautiful, faithful, sincere wife, whose sole care would be her husband's wellbeing, or a timid and loving fiancée.

Then, other thoughts occurred to them and they hesitated, comparing the advantages of the various metamorphoses.

However, the enchanter cried: "Well, have you decided? You're taking too long to reflect, and I don't have time to waste. What do you want to be? Come on, it's necessary to choose—speak, quickly."

There was another long silence, but finally:

"Let me, then," said Abonde, "be the wine that is drunk in suburban taverns. For, better than the bread of alms and the warmth of stoves, and repose in a bed, consolatory intoxication charms weary bodies and hearts."

"Let me," said Myrtile, "be the strings of an old village fiddler's violin. For even more than gilded garments replacing rags, the flight of menacing clouds, and the return home of lost children, the song that makes people dance is good for the poor."

"Let me," said Caricine, "be the beautiful gypsy girl of the crossroads, who offers passers-by her laughter and kisses. For it's in free, foolish, fickle and hazardous amour, devoid of deceptions and regrets, that men forget the ennui or despair of living."

Since that time, Abonde laughs in full glasses on the tables of taverns, and Myrtile makes people dance at country weddings under the trees of the main square or the courtyard of an inn; they are happy, the fallen good fays, with the joy they provide, but they are also jealous—jealous of Caricine, because they know full well that she is the one who provides the best charity.

THE BONNET COLLECTOR

I AM in a position to provide news of Puck to persons curious to know what has become of him since he quit the wood near Athens. It was generally supposed—and I was inclined to that error myself—that, punished for some overly hazardous mischief, he was languishing in exile in an orchard in the isles of Avalon; people who claimed to be well-informed recounted that he had committed the imprudence of falling asleep one evening in an amorous rose, and that the rose, having closed, did not open again. Other gossips spread other stories.

Everyone was mistaken. The truth is that the companion of Peasblossom and Mustardseed has never ceased living among humans. I encountered him, one morning in spring, in a hawthorn grove, suspended, like a gymnast from a trapeze, from a tremulous thread of a spider-web. But he has rendered himself somewhat different from the Robin Goodfellow of old; it is no longer him who whinnies like a coquettish filly in order to deceive a sturdy horse nourished on beans; it is no longer him who insinuates himself into a housewife's bowl and adopts the exact form of a cooked apple, or who offers a stool to a stout matron, and suddenly snatches it away so that she falls on her backside, to the great merriment of the assembly.

No, Puck has more serious concerns now; he is fulfilling a grave function; he is, by trade, a collector of bonnets from the other side of the windmill.[1]

To begin with, the confession of that profession, apparently rather strange, could not fail to surprise me; I was tempted to believe that Robin was making fun of me. It is well-known that he has no great pleasure than making fun of people; it is not always necessary to take him at his word. After reflection, however, I was forced to admit that such a métier might exist, and that it would even be inexplicable if it did not exist.

For, after all, I ask you, when you walk behind windmills, or in the surrounding pathways, have you ever seen any bonnets? No, you've never seen any—on the ground, I mean. As for those that are perceived on top of the tousled brown or red hair of lovely girls going by, nothing, thank God, is more frequent. But of bonnets fallen in the grass, or hanging on branches, one does not notice any. It is, however, averred that a considerable number of them are flung every day—and every night—and one would be treading all the time on frills, lace and straw, as a birdcatcher tramples doves, if someone were not picking up the bonnets.

Truly, I was quite crestfallen not to have thought a long time ago about the necessity of that function; I might perhaps have solicited it, although there must be something

1. In English, "flinging (or throwing) one's cap (or bonnet) over the windmill" means behaving recklessly or flouting convention; the phrase is sometimes said to derive from *Don Quixote*, although that must be reckoned dubious. Its French equivalent tends to be more restricted, referring specifically to young women recklessly losing their virginity.

painful, and also humiliating, in observing the fall of so much modesty and innocence, when one has had nothing to do with it. The charming thing is not picking up a bonnet after it has caused its wounded bird to stumble; it is untying the strings. Anyway, regrets would be futile, since Puck is in position and shows no desire to hand in his resignation, in spite of the great trouble he is obliged to take.

"You can't imagine," he told me, "how taxing the employment to which I've devoted myself is. I can no longer find time to chat beside springs with the reed-warblers, or laugh with the babbling brooks, or make war against the scarabs in order the steal the armor of their wings in order to make a beautiful breast-plate. As soon as I begin unlacing the green corset of a rosebud, my duty obliges me to run hither and yon, and the young roses hold a grudge against me for only being half-undressed, being just like women, who absolutely insist on one finishing whatever one has started.

"Oh, it's very fortunate that it only takes me a quarter of a third of a second to fly from one end of the earth to the other, because, almost simultaneously, in all lands, bonnets are flying and landing. Recently, especially, in truth, I don't know which way to turn. A snowstorm of headgear is flapping its wings above windmills, hesitating, and then falling. The day before yesterday, I was virtually buried beneath a light avalanche. I picked up twenty bonnets and a thousand fell, and more were still falling! I thought I was going to choke—but such a death wouldn't have displeased me, among the ribbons, the batiste and the Mechlin lace, because of that odor of hair and napes, so intoxicating, as you know."

"But Robin," I said to Puck, "there's one thing that I don't understand. You pick up the bonnets, all well and good; but once they're picked up, where do you put them? If you have the custom of arranging them on shelves or in drawers, as good housekeepers do, you must have a very large number of cupboards and chests of drawers."

Puck burst out laughing.

"Three million cabinet-makers working for three million years wouldn't be sufficient to make enough chests of drawers and cupboards for one to be able to put away all the bonnets thrown over windmills, even packing them in tightly. Come with me, and you'll see something that can't fail to interest you."

When one travels with Puck, one travels very quickly; a *belle-de-nuit* could only open half way in the time it took us to go from the arbor where we were to a strange vast garden, so vast that you would have thought it only a little less large than the entire earth. And that garden, full of innumerable interlaced trees, had, instead of hyacinths, roses, camellias and carnations, adorable little bonnets that were quivering in the wind. It was reminiscent of an immense Eden crossed with a milliner's boutique.

I saw canvas bonnets devoid of ribbons or flowers, hanging from hawthorns; the bonnets of poor girls that had taken flight during harvest time after a false step behind a corn-mill. There were guipure bonnets, valencienne bonnets, flourishing with white-rose and opoponax; bonnets that were the head-dresses of nuns, and retained, along with an odor of incense, a resemblance to lilies; there were also, more impossible to number than the stars in the sky or the grains of sand in Nubia, bonnets that, instead of being bonnets, were hats, veils, corsets, skirts and chemises. For the respect of a proverbial metaphor has limits, after all; one can't demand of young women who want to throw their bonnet over the windmill that they always have a bonnet to hand; one throws what one can.

Meanwhile, my soul mellowing, I thought of all the kisses given and received in the woods, in back alleys, in cloisters, in boudoirs, and I admired Woman and Man, the whole of loving humanity.

"Yes," Puck went on, "this garden is pleasant. One experiences some satisfaction in walking along its paths; it was a good idea I had to hang the previous day's bonnets on the bushes every morning."

"The previous day's?" I exclaimed, amazed. "You don't mean, I assume, that what you're showing me here is a single day's harvest?"

"Yes, that is what I mean, and what I said. As soon as dawn breaks, I replace the old bonnets with the new ones. Yesterday wasn't very good, relatively speaking."

O joy! O pride! O infinity of amour! How many hearts changed! How many souls mingled! How many mouths on mouths! How good the gods are!

When I had recovered from my ecstasy, I said to Puck: "In that case, you owe me another explanation. Where do you put yesterday's bonnets, the day before yesterday's, and those from before, indefinitely, Robin Goodfellow?"

"Where do I put them? Everywhere! And soon, there won't be any more room there."

He continued, while amusing himself by making a ladybird climb on to the little finger of his left hand: "I make them into other bonnets for the ingenues with hearts as yet untroubled, and they soon come back to me, already knowing the way. I make them into wedding-chemises and nuptial bedsheets for the amorous women who sanctify their sin by becoming wives. I make them into ball-gowns that counsel, by their rustling, the abandonments of the waltz, into curtains for alcoves, and I also make them—for I don't know where else to hide them—into tablecloths and altar-cloths. But it wouldn't be sufficient, in order to employ them all, to dress all the women and all the men, to decorate all the apartments, to ornament all the temples.

"I even mingle them with nature in order to get rid of them. Thanks to me, they flower in eglantines, scatter in rainstorms, condense in morning dew and spin out in threads of spidersilk; I tear them up into butterflies that love roses, remembering lips; birds make use of them to make their nests softer; their muslin shivers in the morning mists, gliding over the meadows; it's their pale ribbons that unwind in the interminable lengths of long flat roads, their blue and green ribbons that extend in the smooth extension of rivers; when it snows, anyone who knows these things will recognize their whiteness in the light flakes.

"In consequence, you live, you humans, without knowing it, in the midst of so many bonnets that have become flowers, hailstorms, dewdrops, butterflies, soft nests, distant mists, fleeting water and gentle snow! And when I've finished filling the terrestrial world with them, I fill the sky with them, with those bonnets. They're the aurora—those of young girls—and the evening dusk—those of old women, which linger for a long time; they're the rose and the azure of the mysterious profundities; they burn in the sun, pale in the moon, travel with comets, blaze in meteors; and it's of bonnets thrown over windmills—scattered, swarming whitenesses—that the Milky Way is made."

THE THREE SOWERS

THREE young companions were traveling the world. As it was winter, it was raining, blowing and snowing over all the surrounding countries, but the road they were going along was gilded by sunlight, and the clumps of flowering hawthorn shook off, in every gust of the breeze, flocks of butterflies and bees, because they were children of sixteen. In order that spring should smile around travelers, it is sufficient that they have it within them; on the contrary, if an old man enters an April garden on a rosy morning, the daylight fades, the sky is veiled, and the pale eglantines are little flakes of snow.

So, they were going along without knowing where, and that is the best way of following one's path. One was named Honorat, another Chrysor, and the youngest was named Aloys. All three were handsome, with curly hair, which the wind uncurled, with youthful health in their cheeks and mouths.

Seeing them walking along the sunlit road, you would have had difficulty finding any difference between them; however, Honorat had the most arrogant air about him, Chrysor the most cunning, and Aloys the most timid. What they seemed externally, they were within. The body is only the lining of the soul, but humans have the bad habit of wearing their natural clothing inside out.

Honorat, in his chimeras, could not help imagining that he was the son of some powerful king. A famished client of the Hazard Inn, eating crusts of bread thrown out of the window by the satiety of rich folk, drinking water from spring in the hollow of his hand, and sleeping in the shelter of barns, it made no difference: he saw himself enveloped by sumptuousness and glory. What he dreamed about were courtiers, dazzling in their gaudy garments, kneeling in the throne-room between colonnades of jasper or porphyry; through a great double door, wide-open, ambassadors came in, sent from the most distant countries, while behind them were African slaves clad in red satin carrying coffers in which were heaped, marvelous and charming, precious stones, fine pearls, silk and brocade fabrics, the humble tributes of the Emperor of Trebizond and the King of Srinagar. Or he imagined that he was leading innumerable armies to victory, which he plunged, his sword in the sunlight, into the routed masses of enemy troops, and that his people bore him in triumph under arches decorated with fluttering banners in which the wings of glory beat.

Chrysor, for his part, had less epic dreams. Coins, a great many coins, always coins, silver and gold, particularly gold, and countless diamonds, of which one alone was worth all the treasures of the richest of monarchs: that was what sparkled before his eyes, what streamed between his fingers, at the very moment when he held out his hand to passers-by, glad to receive a copper sou. If he were to be placed between two doors, that of paradise and that of a strong-box, it is not the one to paradise that he would have opened.

As for little Aloys—prettier and frailer than his companions—he did not worry about palaces, courtiers, ambassadors or armies; to a table laden with gold he would have preferred a corner of a flowering meadow. With his adolescent, almost effeminate air, he readily lowered his attentive eyes to the ladybirds scaling the blades of grass, only raising them to admire the redness of juvenile auroras on the horizon, or that of pensive sunsets. The only joy he desired—and he had it—was to sing while he walked the song that he had sung the day before, a song with beautiful rhymes, which the birds approved, in the bushes along the roadside, by repeating the refrain.

In consequence, if, in the evenings, in the bright silence of the stars, one of those rumors awoke, grew and died that are the sighs of sleeping nature. Honorat asked: "Isn't that the echo of the sound of trumpets?" and Chrysor said: "Isn't it the distant sound of a gold coin falling out of a drawer?" but Aloys murmured "I think it's the little chirping of a bird's nest going back to sleep."

One day, an old woman saw them coming, while she was digging very small furrows in a field with her spade, in order to sow seeds therein. She was so old and so ill-dressed that you might have taken her for an ancient centenarian dressed in rags, and her antiquity was complicated by ugliness. One eye punctured, all yellow, the other half-covered by a leucoma; three tufts of gray hair tucked under a dirty cotton headscarf; red skin with warts, and lips flapping loosely for want to teeth every time she breathed, she had everything necessary to make the gaze despair.

Any man who went past her would have hastened his pace, devoured by the need to see a beautiful girl or a rose. But who would assume the task of writing fairy tales if he did not have the right to transform, in the course of his tales, the most hideous individuals into young ladies dazzling with beauty and adornments? It is well-known that in our stories, the more repulsive one is to begin with, the more beautiful one will be in a little while. The toothless centenarian never fails to conform to the poetics of the worthy Perrault and Madame d'Aulnoy.

When the three companions, Honorat, Chrysor and Aloys, perceived her from the edge of the ditch, the old woman had changed into the most adorable fay one could ever see, and the flounces of her dress were so florid with flowers of precious stones that butterflies were fluttering around her, all thinking that the month of April had blossomed in that meager field.

"Stop, handsome lads," said the fay. "I wish you well, because you're young—which is the most charming fashion of being good—and because you always take care, while waking, not to crush the insects that are crossing the road. I invite you to come here, and sow what you will in the furrows I have dug. You have the word of a good fay that this ugly field, more fecund than it seems, will render you a hundredfold anything that you wish to give it."

You can imagine that the travelers were charmed to see such a beautiful person and to hear such obliging words. At the same time, though, they found themselves very embarrassed, being poor to the point that they had nothing at all to sow in the magic furrow.

"Alas, Madame," said Honorat, after having conferred with Chrysor and Aloys, "we don't possess anything that we would like to see returned a hundredfold, except for our dreams, which won't germinate."

"How do you know?" she said, smiling, brushing away with a flick of her hair a butterfly that had settled on her ear—it had the excuse that the ear resembled a carnation. "Who can tell, careless youths? Sow your dreams in the open earth, and we'll see what grows."

Then Honorat, kneeling down, with his mouth to the furrow, commenced relating his ambitious chimeras: the palaces of porphyry and jasper in which the gaudy courtiers were resplendent, and the ambassadors entering through the regal door, and negroes laden with tributes, and armies and triumphs.

He did not have time to finish. Galloping cavaliers raced over the plain, numerous and armored in gold, plumed with eagle feathers, proclaiming that they were seeking the son of the deceased king, in order to take him to his throne. As soon as they had perceived Honorat they cried: "Its him!" and, full of joy, they bore their master away toward beautiful marble dwellings, battles and trophies.

Having seen that, Chrysor did not have to be begged to sow in the soil his desire for riches, his love of sharply ringing coins and precious stones. He had scarcely pronounced a few words when the furrow was filled with gold, silver, diamonds and pearls. He threw himself on to them, seized them, filled his pockets with them, and his mouth too, and fled, richer than the richest of men, seeking some safe hiding place in which to bury his treasures.

"Well," asked the fay, "what do you think, Aloys? Aren't you going to follow the example of your companions?"

He did not reply at first, having scarcely paid any heed to what had happened, occupied with a marriage of myrtles in a tangle of convolvulus.

"Well," he said, finally, "I don't desire anything except to listen to the plaints of nightingales in the dusk, and the crickets that screech in the warm noonday. All that I could do would be to sing an epithalamium into the furrow, which I composed yesterday for the wedding of two warblers."

"Sing it," replied the fay. "That seed is worth as much as many another."

As he began the second verse, a beautiful young woman, semi-naked, so beautiful that no amorous dream ever wished for one more perfect, emerged from the parted earth and put her two arms, lianas for enlacement and lilies for whiteness, around the neck of the delighted youth.

"Oh, how well you sing!" she said to him. "I love you."

It was thus that the good fay came to the aid of the three vagabond children, who were following the sunlit road without knowing where it led.

A short time after that, however, terrible events occurred.

Vanquished in a battle, after prodigies of courage, by implacable enemies, King Honorat was obliged to quit his capital and take refuge in a cloister, where his hair was cut, not without having removed his crown.

Thieves, who are always on the lookout, ended up discovering the hiding place where Chrysor the Rich had buried his treasures, and he was reduced, in rags, to wandering the roads, asking his robbers for alms, which they did not give him.

Only Aloys did not cease to be happy, kissed by the sun in the morning, and from morning to evening by the beautiful young woman whose arms, as supple as lianas, were as white as lilies; and she was faithful to him always, forever, because he had sung into the furrow a well-rhymed song.

THE BEAUTY
WITH THE HEART OF SNOW

THERE was in a kingdom a princess so beautiful that, in the opinion of everyone, nothing as perfect had ever been seen on earth. It was, however, quite unnecessary that she was pretty, because she did not want to love anyone. In spite of the pleas of her parents, she refused scornfully all the parties that were proposed to her. When the nephews or sons of emperors came to the court to ask or her hand, she did not even deign to look at them, no matter how young and handsome they were. She turned her head away with an expression of disgust.

"Truly, it wasn't worth the trouble of disturbing me for so little."

Eventually, because of the coldness that she showed on every occasion, the princess had been nicknamed "the Beauty with the heart of snow." In vain, her nurse, a worthy old woman who had a great deal of experience, said to her, with tears in her eyes:

"Be careful of what you're doing, my girl. It's not an honest thing only to respond with nasty remarks to people who love you with all their hearts. What! Among so many handsome young men, so well-dressed, who are yearning to obtain you in marriage, there isn't even one for whom you experience some tender sentiment? Be careful I tell you; the good fays, by whom you've been accorded an incomparable beauty, will become irritated one day or another if you continue to be miserly with your gift; what they have given you, they want you to give; the more you're worth, the more you owe; it's necessary to measure alms to wealth. What will become of you, my child, if your protectresses, annoyed by your indifference, abandon you to the malevolence of certain fays who rejoice in evil, and are always prowling, with bad intentions, around young princesses?"

The Beauty with the heart of snow took no account of this good advice; she shrugged her shoulders and looked at herself in a mirror; and that was sufficient for her.

As for the King and Queen, they were more desolate than one can say at the indifference in which their daughter was obstinate; they came to think that an evil genius had put a spell on her. They had it proclaimed by heralds that they would give the princess herself to the man who could deliver her from the spell of which she was the victim.

✦✦✦

Now, at that time, in a great forest, there was a woodcutter, very hideous to behold, deformed, and lame because of the weight of his hump, who was the terror of the entire region—for often he did not limit himself to chopping down trees; lying in ambush in some ravine, he waited with his ax raised for some unsuspecting traveler, and severed his head as skillfully as the most experienced executioner would have done. After that, he searched the cadaver, and, with the money he found in the pockets, he bought food and wine, on which he gorged himself in his hut, uttering loud cries of joy.

114

In consequence, that evil man was happier than many honest folk, as long as travelers were passing through his forest. But it was soon of such ill repute that even the boldest individuals made long detours rather than traverse it; the woodcutter was idle. For several weeks he lived as best he could on the remains of his old feasts, gnawing the bones and pouring the dregs of poorly emptied bottles into his cup. It was meager fare for a glutton and a drunkard like him.

The rigor of winter brought his misfortune to a peak. In his lair, through which the wind blew, where snowflakes settled, he was dying of cold as well as hunger. As for going to ask for help from the inhabitants of the nearest village, he could not think of that because of the hatred he had attracted.

You might think: *Why didn't he make a fire with faggots and dry brushwood?* Well, because the wood, like the leaves, was so penetrated by frost that there was no means of setting it alight. One might also suppose that, in order to punish the vile man, an unknown will prevented the fire from catching. At any rate, the woodcutter spent exceedingly sad days and even sadder nights, beside his empty bread-bin, before his black hearth; on seeing him thin and shivering, you would not have failed to pity him, if you had been unaware of how he had merited his misery by his crimes.

However, someone took pity on him. It was a wicked fairy named Melandrine. As it pleased her to see evil, it was natural that she liked those who did it.

One night, therefore, when he was utterly desolate, his teeth chattering, his fingers frostbitten and he would have sold his soul—which, to tell the truth, was not worth much—for a flaming vine-branch, Melandrine appeared to him, emerging from underground.

She was not beautiful and blonde with garlands of flowers in her hair; she was not wearing a brocade robe resplendent with gems. Ugly, bald, and also hump-backed, as ragged as a pauperess, you would have taken her for an old vagabond beggar; for if one is wicked, one cannot appear beautiful, even if one is a fay.

"Don't despair, poor man," she said. "I want to come to your aid. Follow me."

Somewhat astonished by that apparition, he marched behind Melandrine to a clearing where there was a heap of snow.

"Now light the fire," she said.

"Eh! Snow doesn't burn, Madame!"

"That's where you're wrong. Here, take this wand of dogwood, which I've brought for you. It will suffice for you to touch one of these great white heaps with it, to have the most beautiful fire that has ever been seen.

He did as she had said. Imagine his astonishment! Scarcely had the branch touched it than the snow caught fire, as if had had been, not snow, but tinder. The entire clearing was illuminated by flames.

From that moment on, the woodcutter, while continuing to be hungry, at least no longer knew the suffering of being cold; as soon as he felt a little shiver, he made a heap of snow in his hut or on the road, and then touched it with the wand that Melandrine had given him, and warmed himself in front of a good fire.

❦

A few days after that adventure, there was a great agitation in the capital of the neighboring kingdom. The courtyard of the palace was full of halberdiers who were making their halberds ring on the flagstones. But it was in the throne-room above all that the emotion was great. The most powerful princes of the earth, with many other young men, had gathered together here in order to attempt, in a courteous battle, finally to move the Beauty with the heart of snow.

The nephew of the Emperor of Trebizond bent his knee.

"I command more armed men than there are leaves in all the forests, and I have in my coffers more pearls than there are stars in the sky. Would you like, O Princess, to reign over my people and adorn yourself with my pearls?"

"What did he say?" asked the princess.

In his turn, the son of the King of Mataquin knelt down.

"Although still young. I have vanquished the most illustrious knights in tournaments, and, with a single sweep of the sword, I have cut off the hundred heads of a tarasque that was devouring all the newborns and virgins of my kingdom. O Princess, would you like to share my glory, which will increase further?"

"He was speaking so quietly," said the princess, "that I didn't hear him."

And other princes, after the heir to Trebizond and the heir to Mataquin, boasted of their power, their wealth and their glory. Then, bowing, with tender words, came poets who played the guitar as seraphim play the harp, knights who had defended the honor of ladies in the most perilous combats, and also young pages, trembling, roses of modesty, whose lips quivered in the hope of a kiss.

But the Beauty with the heart of snow said: "What do all these people want? Tell them to go away; I don't want to endure their chatter any longer, and I'm in haste to be alone in order to look at myself in my mirror."

"Oh, my girl, my girl," said the nurse, "beware of irritating the good fays!"

Then a rustic lout came forward, very hideous to behold, deformed, and lame because of the weight of his hump. The courtiers who were at the foot of the throne tried to send him away, mocking the peasant who was involving himself in pretending to the hand of a royal person. However, he continued to approach, and, with a wand that he had in his hand, touched the corsage of the indifferent child.

"Oh, how I love him!" she cried, sensing her entire being light up and melt in tenderness.

You can imagine the uproar that followed.

But a king only has his word; the father of the princess had to let her go with the wicked woodcutter to the ill-famed forest.

She lived there very unhappily, for her amour did not blind her to the extent of concealing from her how unworthy the man who had inspired it was; and that was the punishment of the Beauty with the heart of snow.

THE TWO DAISIES

L AMBERT AND LANDRY, who were not fortu-
nate in their family, being the sons of very poor folk,
resolved to go out into the world in order to seek their
fortune. It was on a spring morning that they set forth.
Landry was fifteen, Lambert sixteen; they were, therefore,
very young to wander in that fashion; along with a great
deal of hope, they had a little anxiety, but they were sin-
gularly comforted by an adventure that befell them at the
very start of their journey.

As they were going along the edge of a little wood,
a lady came to meet them. She was completely adorned
with flowers; buttercups and pimpernels were smiling in
her hair; the convolvulus that garlanded her dress fell all
the way to her dainty shoes of moss, like green velvet;
her lips resembled an eglantine and her eyes cornflowers
Every time she moved, butterflies fluttered around her in
a sprinkling of dew. And it was not surprising that she was
like that, because she was the fay Primavera, who is seen
in April passing with a song through the greening woods
and the flowering meadows.

"Well," she said to the two brothers, "since you're de-
parting on a long journey, I want to make each of you a
gift. Landry, accept this daisy, and you, Lambert, a daisy

also. It will be sufficient for you to detach a petal from these flowers and throw it away to experience at that very instant an unparalleled joy, which will be precisely what you will have desired. Go, follow your road, and try to make good use of Primavera's gifts."

They thanked the obliging fay very politely, and then set forth again, as satisfied as possible. But when they reached a crossroads, there was a disagreement between them. Lambert wanted to go to the right, Landry wanted to go to the left; with the consequence that, in order to put an end to the quarrel, each one did as he wished and they separated, after having embraced one another. Perhaps each brother was not sorry to be alone, in order to use more freely the gift that the lady clad in flowers had given him.

❦

On entering the next village, Landry perceived a young woman leaning on a window-sill, and he had difficulty holding back an exclamation, so pretty did she seem. No, he had never seen such a charming person; he had never even dreamed that her like existed. Almost still a child, with hair so light and blonde that one could scarcely distinguish it from the sunlit air, she had a pale complexion here, and a slight blush there: lily-white on the forehead, rosy on the cheeks; her eyes opened like the blossoming of a periwinkle in which a raindrop was shining; there were no lips that, in proximity with hers, would not have wanted to be bees.

Landry did not hesitate. He tore off and threw away one of the petals of his daisy.

120

The wind had not yet carried away the frail debris when the child from the window was in the street, smiling at the traveler. They went toward the nearby wood, hand in hand, talking in low voices, saying that they loved one another; merely by hearing that, they experienced such delights that they thought they were in paradise.

And they knew many moments similar to that first moment, many days as sweet as that first day. It would have been happiness without end had the child not died one day in autumn, while the withered leaves, sent flying by the bitter wind, struck windows with little taps, like the light fingers of Death passing by.

Landry wept for a long time, but tears do not blind one to the extent that one cannot look through them. Once, he saw a passing beauty clad in gold satin, her eyes bold and her lips madcap; and, throwing another petal to the wind, he departed with her.

From then on, insouciant, asking every hour to be a joy and every joy to last no longer than an hour, relentlessly infatuated with that which charms, excites and ecstasizes, he spent days and nights, without counting them, in all laughter and all kisses. The breeze hardly had time to stir the branches of rose-bushes and lift the veils of women, being always occupied in carrying away the petals of the daisy.

※❧❧❧※

Lambert's conduct was entirely different. He was an economical young fellow incapable of squandering his treasure. As soon as he found himself alone on the road he made himself a promise to conserve the fay's present. For, after all, numerous as the petals of the corolla were, a day would come when he would have no more of them if he tore them off at every opportunity. Prudence demanded that he keep them for the future; by acting in that fashion he would certainly conform to Primavera's intentions.

In the first town through which he passed he bought a very solid little box, which closed with a key; it was in there that he put the flower, resolved never to look at it; he wanted to avoid temptation. It would have been to commit a sin for him to raise his eyes toward young women at windows or to follow passing beauties with illuminated gazes and madcap lips.

Reasonable and methodical, worrying about serious things, he became a merchant, and made a lot of money. He had nothing but scorn for the thoughtless individuals who spent their time in enjoyment, without any concern for the morrow; when the opportunity presented itself, he never failed to reprimand them soundly. Thus, he was highly esteemed by honest folk; they were in accord in praising him, offering him as an example. And he continued to grow rich, working from dawn to dusk.

To tell the truth, he was not happy, as he would have liked to be; he could not help thinking about the joys that he was refusing himself. He would only have had to open the little box and throw a petal to the wind to love and be loved. But he repressed those dangerous whims every time. He had plenty of time. He would know joy later. Would he be any further forward, when his daisy was stripped of its petals? *Patience: let's not hurry!* He would risk nothing by waiting, since the flower was safe in the box.

The breeze, prowling around him, murmured: "Throw me a petal, throw, in order that I can take it away and you can smile!" but he turned a deaf ear to it; and the wind went off to stir the branches of the rose-bushes and tickle the cheeks of young women with the lace of veils.

⁂

Many years later, it happened one day that Lambert, while visiting his properties, encountered in the country a rather badly-dressed man walking alongside a field of alfalfa.

"Oh!" he said. "What do I see? Isn't that you, Landry, my brother?"

"It's really me," the other replied.

"What a sorry state I find you in! You lead me to believe that you have made poor use of Primavera's gift."

"Alas," sighed Landry, "perhaps I threw all the petals to the wind too quickly. However, although a little sad, I don't repent my imprudence. I've had so many joys, my brother!"

"It's done you a lot of good! If you'd been as circumspect as me, you wouldn't be reduced to sterile regrets. For, know that I only have to make a gesture to enjoy all the pleasures from why you have been weaned."

"Is it possible?"

"Undoubtedly, since I've kept the fay's gift intact. Ha ha! I can give myself a good time if I wish! That's what comes of being economical."

"What! Intact, truly?"

"Take a look," said Lambert, opening the box that he had taken out of his pocket.

But he went very pale, for, instead of the fresh blooming daisy, there was nothing before his eyes but a little gray heap of dust, like a pinch of funereal ash.

123

"Oh!" he cried, angrily. "A curse on the wicked fay who has tricked me!"

Then a young lady, all dressed in flowers, emerged from a bush by the roadside.

"I haven't tricked you or your brother," she said, "and it's time to explain things to you. The two daisies were not, in fact, flowers, they were your youth itself: your youth, Landry, which you threw to the winds of caprice, and your youth, Lambert, which you allowed to wither, without making use of it, in your ever-closed heart—and you don't even have what remains to your brother: the memory of having stripped the flower of its petals."

THE LAME ANGEL

ONE morning in summer when he was walking in the snow—for in that land, it snows in the middle of summer under the lukewarm sun, and the flakes, white without being cold, stick to the bushes as jasmines and lilies—the son of the King of the Pale Isles saw something diamantine and silvery on the ground, quivering gently like a harp that the fingers of a musician have just quit.

If smaller, that light form, pearly with the tears of the aurora, might have been the wing of a dove, torn away and dropped by the claw of a vulture; but large, with a hint of azure that had doubtless traversed paradises remaining at the tips of its plumes, it was the wing of an angel; there was no mistaking it.

At the sight of it, the King's son felt depressed by melancholy. What! A divine messenger, perhaps in a battle with some tenebrous spirit, perhaps under a gust of infernal wind, had lost one of his wings? Had he committed the imprudence of settling one evening—mistaking the room—near the overly perfumed bed of one of those cruel amorous women who have no more cherished pleasure than bruising that which flies, and plucking the feathers from illusions? A single caress or a woman's breath is often sufficient to cause a wing to fall.

At any rate, he must be in great pain now. What a humiliation and what sadness for him, on the evenings of those balls at which one dances with the prettiest of the eleven thousand virgins, to be mocked by his celestial brothers, a poor maladroit individual who waltzes poorly, being lame.

Lame? Certainly. Since they are not bodies, but souls with plumage, angels are not lame in the foot, but the wing.

Because of that probable pain, the Prince of the Pale Isles thought dolorously. In his compassion, he could not bear the idea of one of the cherubim or seraphim like a wounded pigeon; and he resolved to return the thing he had found, so white, diamantine, silvery and gently quivering, to the individual who had lost it.

But that was a design easier to conceive than to execute. By what means could an angel regretting his wing be found? One cannot enter as one wishes the paradisal abode. As for posting notices on the walls of cities throughout the real, declaring that whichever of the elohim had lost a precious object could recover it at the royal palace, that would have been futile; angels do not have the habit of strolling in the streets like human idlers. In consequence, the young prince was quite perplexed.

He thought that he ought to consult a little fiancée that he had by virtue of amour, unknown to his parents. She was the daughter of a woodcutter in the forest. With the wing under his arm, he went to see her.

He met her on the edge of the wood, some way in front of the cottage where she lived.

"Oh, dear soul," he said to her, "it's sad news that I'm bringing you."

"What is it, if you please?" she asked.

"An angel has lost one of his white wings."

She blushed, but she did not seem surprised. One might have thought that she was already informed of that distressing event, and when he had added: "I'm determined to return it to him," she lowered her eyes, blushing even more deeply.

"My dear soul," he went on, "you alone can reveal to me how I ought to proceed in order to succeed in my enterprise. You're so pretty and so pure that all the celestial spirits gather by day in your thoughts, and by night in your dreams. It's impossible that, while listening to them, you haven't heard mention of what has happened to one of them."

"Alas," she said, "I'm as well-informed of things as it's possible to be; it is my guardian angel, in fact, who has lost one of his wings."

"Really? Your guardian angel? That's a singular coincidence. Tell me, I beg you, how that misfortune happened to him."

"It was your fault, I assure you! You remember that stroll we took together the other evening, under the lemon-trees, where the stars were trembling like golden fruits?"

"How could I have forgotten it? It was on that evening that you permitted my lips, for the first time, to touch your cheek, and since then, my mouth has been perfumed, as if I had eaten roses,"

"Yes, that evening you gave me a kiss, but if it was sweet for me, it was cruel to the angel who was following me among the branches, to warn me and defend me. One of his wings flew away from him when your caress brushed me. It is the law of the guardians to whom heaven confides young women, to be the first victims of the sins they commit."

"Oh, what a nasty law! I imagine that your angel, crippled, must be very upset."

"More than you can imagine! Downcast, frail, incapable of returning to heaven even if he dared to do so, he is desolate and tearful, and I have the chagrin by night of not dreaming about you, because he prevents me from sleeping by his lamentations."

"It's important then, that we return his wing to him, at all costs. I can't repent of the harm I've done, but I'd nevertheless like there to be a means of repairing it."

"I think that there might be one," she murmured

"Oh! What is it? Tell me quickly!"

"It would be necessary,"—she was speaking so quietly that he could hardly hear her—"to return things to the state in which they were prior to the walk under the beautiful lemon-trees. My angel lost his wing because I received your kiss; he would doubtless recover it if . . ."

"If? Go on to the end, please."

"If I return it to you!"

As she said those words, quivering, with modesty in her cheeks, she was reminiscent of a mimosa that would like to be a rose; and as the prince approached her, ecstatic at the means that she had imagined, she fled through the branches, which, shaken, scattered gold and diamond droplets in the sunlight.

He ran after her, caught up with her, and obliged her to sit down at the foot of a myrtle taller than the tall oaks; in the profound mystery of the woods, amid the silence of nests where the birds fell silent in order to listen, he spoke to her on his knees, as one prays in a temple.

"You whom I love, you whom I adore, why flee from me, after saying that? Have you only given me the hope of your lips on my cheek in order to leave me, more bitter, the despair of not having felt them pose there softly? Oh, how delighted the flowers are when the flight of a tremulous butterfly settles there! It's delight that ripples the water striped by dragonflies; one cannot imagine the joy of foliage brushed by a dove. But how much happier I would be than the flower where the butterfly settles, and the wave beneath the tremor of damsel-flies, and the foliage caressed by plumage, if your mouth—oh, your mouth!—brushed me with its rosy breath!

She made no reply, turning her head away, not wanting to see the dear face of the child, blossoming like the morning, on which she would have taken so much pleasure in placing a long kiss.

He continued speaking, sadly:

"It is, therefore, that you're very cruel, since you don't want to! I could understand that you might refuse me the incomparable joy that I implore if it were only a matter of me, whom you do not love enough. But wicked girl, you are not thinking, then, about your angel who is weeping for his white wing? Have you forgotten that in restituting to me the kiss received, you would be rendering him free flight among the clouds and the stars of his paradise? How unhappy he must be, and how plaintive! He is dragging himself over the ground instead of soaring in the aurorae; accustomed to being resplendent in daylight, he is all gray with dust. Have you ever seen an injured turtle-dove trying to regain its branch, unable to do so? It is that bird he resembles. Oh, the poor fellow! If you have no pity for me, have pity for him, and resign yourself to rendering me happy, in order that he might be!"

It was certainly to that consideration that the hesitant young woman ceded. She judged that her duty ordered her to consent to the happiness of a man, for the sake of an angel's happiness; and slowly, with the delay of things that know they are desired, her lips approached the young cheek in flower. They settled upon it!

A quiver shook the branches. It was the angel taking flight, with two wings, joyfully. But the two wings, which had been white, were now pink, like the two kisses.

PUCK'S TREACHERIES

A YOUNG man in silver armor, the wings of a snowy alerion deployed on his helmet, was riding in the early morning on a white mare. It happened that a beautiful princess, strolling under the flowering apple-trees, saw him over the hedge; she was so excited that she dropped the hyacinth she had in her hand, along with a butterfly that had settled on it.

"In truth," she sighed, "wherever he comes from, and wherever he is going, that cavalier will carry my thoughts with him.

She made a sign bidding him to stop and said: "I love you, you who are passing by. If your desire accords with mine, I will take you to my father, who is the King of this realm, and we shall have a beautiful wedding."

"I don't love you," replied the passer-by.

He followed his road.

The princess opened the gate of the orchard, and started running along the road.

"Where have you come from?" she asked. "And where are you going so early in the morning, you who don't want to marry me?"

"I've come from the city where my beloved lives, and I'm going to meet my rival, who is arriving this evening."

"Who is your beloved?"

"The daughter of a vavasour; she spins at her window, singing a song to which the birds listen."

"Who is your rival?"

"The nephew of the Emperor of Golconda. When he draws his sword, one could believe that the sky was thundery, because one sees lightning flashes."

"What did you say when you were with your beloved?"

"I said to her: 'Give me your heart.' She refused it to me."

"What will you say when you encounter your rival?"

"I shall say: 'I want your blood.' It will be necessary for him to give it to me."

"How fearful I am of seeing yours shed! Oh, permit me to go with you."

"The only one by whom it would please me to be accompanied is in her abode at present."

"Let me climb up on to the rump of the horse behind you; I won't ask any more of you."

"Men are not accustomed to going into battle with a woman on the rump of their horse."

And the cavalier spurred his white mare. The King's daughter wept, unhappy forever. As it was early in morning, the sun opened on the horizon an eye still bleary with shadow, and the finches and the linnets woke up and twittered amid the foliage, planning pleasure-parties through the spring woods.

❧❦❧

Puck emerged from an azalea bush, clad in two clover-leaves joined together with maidenhair. He was so small that the costume was a trifle large for him. For a fool's cap he had a hedge convolvulus on which was trembling, like a little bell, a half-closed golden bud.

"Yolaine," said Puck, laughing like a bird's nest, "why are you so sad?"

"My only love has gone, and I can't follow him."

"Is your love that handsome young man in silver armor with the wings of a snowy alerion deployed on his helmet, riding over there on a white mare?"

"That's him. His eyes are as blue as the sky and he has hair the color of the night."

Puck shook the hawthorn branch that was his fool's bauble.

"When it pleases me, Yolaine, the idle tortoise overtakes the clouds, and runaway stallions, suddenly slowed, run less rapidly than the beetle that takes an hour to traverse the leaf of a plane-tree. Yolaine, follow your love without anxiety. Where he's going, you'll arrive at the same time as him."

While Puck went back into the azalea bush, Yolaine set forth. The pebbles on which she set her pretty feet shod in satin and pearls said, with a pretty sound: "Thank you, Yolaine's little feet."

✻✺✻

But the malicious Puck, who delights in such games, had deceived the princess. In vain she walked all day and all evening; she did not catch up with the cavalier whose eyes were as blue as the sky. At midnight, however, on the road, she saw a great white phantom pass by on a spectral horse.

"Oh! Who are you, passing form?" asked Yolaine.

133

"I was a handsome young man with hair the color of night; now I'm no longer anyone. At a nearby crossroads I met the nephew of the Emperor of Golconda, my rival; we fought, and he killed me."

"Where are you going?" she asked.

"I'm going to the city, to the dwelling where me beloved is asleep."

"You'll give her a great scare! Do you think she'll love you dead when she didn't love you alive? Come with me, who has chosen you; I'll make my bed into a nuptial tomb; I'll go to sleep forever beside you, and we'll have a beautiful funeral."

"No. Tonight, taking advantage of my beloved's sleep, I want to bid her adieu in her dreams. I shall kiss, on her sleeping lips, the dream of her song."

"At least permit me to accompany you; let me climb up on the rump of your horse with you."

"It's not the custom of phantoms to visit their beloved with a woman on the rump of their horse."

And the form vanished. The daughter of the King wept, more desperate than before.

As it was past midnight, the moon, in a melancholy fashion, was silvering the horizon, the fields and the road with a snowy gleam; and the finches and linnets, asleep amid the silence of the foliage, were dreaming about their flights through the spring woods.

※※※

Puck emerged from a clump of asphodels; he was wearing mourning-dress, made with two halves of a black tulip; a little spider-web was the crepe of his fool's cap.

"Yolaine, poor Yolaine," said Puck, "Why are you so desolate?"

"My only love is dead, and I can't follow him."

"Is that your love, the phantom who just went by on the road?"

"That's him. His hair the color of night has been taken away from him, and, for regret of losing his beloved, he has wept away his eyes as blue as the sky."

"I know the herbs that revive and the herbs that kill. Find the body of your preferred, and I'll give you the herb that revives."

"Oh, Puck, you deceived me! But if you deceive when it's a matter of doing good, you tell the truth when it's a matter of doing harm. Give me the herb that kills."

"Take it, then," said the malicious Puck. "As soon as you're dead, you'll rejoin your love, and you'll never be apart again."

He gave her four sprigs of a herb that is known as Simonne in memory of a love story.[1] When Puck had gone back into the clump of asphodels, Yoline raised the herb to her lips and died without suffering.

※豊豊※

But Puck, once again, had deceived the princess. As Yolaine's soul rose toward heaven, she saw a soul that was descending toward hell. By the light of a star she recognized the soul of the handsome young man.

"Where are you going, soul of my only love?"

---

1. This reference might have reminded a contemporary reader of *Simonne* (1832) by Victor Mangin, reprinted in tandem with "L'Amour et les roses" in 1842.

"Alas, alas, I spoke of love to my beloved in her dreams, and my posthumous kisses brushed her mouth like a black butterfly trembling on a rose. I'm damned and I'm going to hell."

"Would you like me to go with you, having died in order to see you again? I'll console you in torments, rally you in weaknesses, love you for all eternity. My love will be the source of calm and resignation offered to the lips of your dolor. Would you like me to go with you?"

"No, only the memory of my beloved ought to accompany me."

And the soul of the handsome young man was lost in the darkness, while the soul of the young woman rose up, alone, toward the frightful paradise.

In the meantime, Puck, satisfied with the success of his tricks, prepared traps in the moss of an oak, with crossed twigs, in which to catch reawakened ladybirds.

TEARS ON THE SWORD

ONCE, when the knight Roland was returning from fighting the Moors, he heard it said by a herdsman, while he was letting his horse take a breather in a Pyrenean gorge, that not far from there an enchanter was rendering himself odious throughout the region by his tyranny and his cruelty.

At that story, the horse pricked up its ears and shook its mane, ready to take to the gallop, for he was not unaware that his master ordinarily left scant interval between the moment when such crimes were revealed to him and the one in which he punished the culpable. But the administrator of justice, patient this time, interrogated the mountain shepherd at length. He learned many strange things.

The evil magician, who lived in a castle beside the sea, did not limit himself to robbing travelers, devastating the countryside, setting fire to villages, murdering old men and raping young women; he triumphed over all the noble individuals who came to challenge him, with the intention of putting an end to so much barbarity. He had made the most valiant bite the dust; even by flight they could not escape death. In front of the tower, beaten on one side by the furious sea, there was an enormous heap of bones gnawed by beasts and bleached by the rain; and a flock of crows, soaring and circling beneath the sky, always put a black banner at the summit of the tower.

The worthy Roland could not help laughing. How could he believe that a wicked sorcerer had vanquished paladins armored in iron, with sword or lance in hand? Either the storyteller did not know what he was talking about, or those who had challenged the lord of the tower were cowards unworthy of the name of knight, little pages who had put on battle-dress in order to play.

"Good sire," said the herdsman, "it is not by means of his courage that the enchanter gets the better of all his enemies; he has invented, thanks to his infernal science, an unknown weapon that kills at a distance, without any danger to the killer."

"What?" said Roland, full of surprise and sensing disgust rising to his lips, as if he had swallowed rotten meat.

The shepherd continued: "He takes care not to descend into the plain to face his combatants, for he knows that if he offered his breast, even covered with bronze, a point would not take long to pierce it. He remains hidden behind his wall or behind the heap of bones; then, from his hiding place, with an abrupt sound, a flame suddenly emerges, and without having had time to say a *Pater*, the knight who was advancing with confidence falls to the ground, with a red wound in his throat or forehead."

"By Jesus, vanquisher of Tervagant!"[1] exclaimed Charlemagne's nephew. "I never heard mention of such a cowardly fashion of acting! It's truly very fortunate that I

---

1. Tervagant, or Termagant, is a god attributed to Saracens in Medieval Christian poetry, with no apparent equivalent in actual Muslim belief or mythology.

stopped in this wild place to let my horse take a breather, for I think that before tomorrow, if the saints lend me assistance and the dwelling isn't too far away, I shall have punished the traitor whose life is an offense to God. But is it known—speak frankly—how and of what this diabolical weapon is made?"

"It is said that it consists of a rather long tube, at one end of which a fragment of saltpeter is ignited, and from the other end, a metal ball emerges that cleaves through the air, goes right to its target, and strikes with the rapidity of a thunderbolt."

Roland did not ask any more; he gathered his bridles, squeezed with his knees, where the iron joints grated, and the horse, his mane flying, galloped toward the seashore. But the knight lowered his head sadly during that ride. It was repugnant to him to have to soil his sword with the blood of a coward.

It was the first time that he had gone into combat without pleasure.

❧

The clouds in the west were red above the sea when the castle appeared; one might have imagined that it was all the crimes committed before those stones that were bloodying the horizon. Roland stopped, gazing at the horrible habitation, toward which rose, beneath the sky black with croaking birds, a pale stairway of skeletons. He looked for a path between the bones; there was none, so numerous and densely-packed were the piled-up human remains. It was impossible to reach the keep without marching over death.

139

Oh, generous combatants, come from all the corners of the world to confront the perfidious enchanter, who have been struck down at a distance in cowardly fashion by an invisible adversary, how Roland, in his soul, mourns you and honors you! How he will suffer to hear your bones, devoid of a sepulcher, cracking beneath the hooves of his horse! At the same time a terrible anger comes to him, the duty of avenging you prevailing over the instinct of respecting you.

He spurred his horse, Durandal in hand.

Then, in the distance, between the stones, there was a spark of light, with a loud noise that rolled from echo to echo; a whistle brushed the cavalier's ear. The sorcerer was making use of his treacherous invention. But he did not have the leisure to use it a second time. Pushed by Roland, who had dismounted from his horse, a door grated, whined and screeched, yawning among crumbled stones, and, seized by the throat and strangled, spitting out his soul in a blasphemy, the enchanter fell on to the flagstones beside his useless weapon, while the knight, scarcely out of breath, smiled, content with himself.

In the meantime the crows flew away from the turret, illuminated by brightness under the sun's adieu; it was as if an oriflamme of golden light were replacing the black banner.

But Roland soon stopped smiling. After having pushed the cadaver away with his foot, he bent down and picked up the weapon. He considered it for a long time, handling it with disgust. It was, in fact, made up of a long tube with two openings; death entered by one and exited from the other. The knight meditated in a melancholy fashion.

When night had fallen completely, he marched toward the sea. A boat was there; he went aboard, cast off the moorings and rowed with his strong arms toward the open sea. The steel of his armor, as his body moved back and forth, gleamed in the starlight.

Where was he going? What voyage was he attempting in the darkness? Weary of the fatigues of war, had he conceived the design of reposing in one of the miraculous isles where beautiful fays caress sleeping knights with their light hands and fan them with large green leaves? Or, informed of some injustice beneath distant skies, had he resolved, faithful to his mission, to cause the trenchant equity of the sword to shine out there, amid the lies and treacheries?

No; he wanted to finish his day's work, still incomplete. The enchanter was lying lifeless, the conquered castle loomed up like the enormous and glorious sepulcher of so many knights vanquished by treason; that was good, but it was not enough. It was necessary that the cowardly weapon with which one struck from afar should disappear forever, incapable of being recovered.

He had thought at first of breaking it, but an evil man might have been able to pick up the fragments, and might have been able to make a similar weapon modeled on the reassembled debris. Hide it under the earth? Who could tell whether someone, one day, might have chanced to disinter it? The surest way was to throw it into the sea by night, far from the shore; that is why he was rowing toward the open sea.

When he was a long way from the shore—a very long way—when he was certain that he could no longer be seen, when he could no longer see anything himself, except for the immensity of the waters and the immensity of the sky, he stood up, took the diabolical weapon in his right hand, spat on it, and threw it into the sea, where it sank very quickly.

Then he remained pensive, his tall stature, blanched by the starlight, slowly stirred by the swell of the waves. He did not feel placated, in spite of what he had done. He told himself that one day or another, in a near or distant future, someone might perhaps take it no his head to invent an apparatus similar to the one that he had thrown into the waves.

He, the knight who rejoiced in lances broken in the encounter of palfreys, the luminous clash of blades, breasts confronting breasts, red wounds proximal to the hands that inflicted them, had the somber vision of a strange war, in which people hated at a distance, in which those who struck blows could not see those whom they struck down, in which the most cowardly could kill the bravest, in which treacherous hazard alone, in the smoke and the noise, disposed of destinies.

Then, considering Durandal, sparkling in the starlight, Roland wept.

He wept for a long time, and his tears fell, one by one, on to the loyal blade of the Sword.

THE LITTLE BLUE FLAME

"YES, lovely child," said the fay, "thanks to the little blue flame that I have put on your forehead, you will be able to triumph over all darkness; you will finally enter, after much effort, the miraculous Garden of Joy and Dreams, which opens its diamond door on the other side of shadow. There, you will live eternally happy, having forgotten the sorrows of the obscure world, breathing a subtle air made of the soul of roses and the bright breath of the stars; and angelic lilies, in thousands, will be the censers of your glory.

"Go, then, through the perils, go without dread and without doubt; no human or diabolical power will be able to prevent you from reaching your goal if you conserve, still alight, the little blue flame. But if it goes out—be carefully not to let it go out!—you will immediately be enveloped by a profound night, and, groping your way, bumping into invisible walls, falling into unanticipated precipices, you will never again find the route to the incomparable garden."

The child thanked the good fay for the present she had made him and the advice she had given him. He set forth along a path of flowers, in the morning sun. The blue flame he had on his forehead was more luminous than the daylight.

He did not take long to encounter potholes in which it would have been very easy to break one's neck. Pebbles rolled under his feet, and, as if by virtue of the echo of the impact, blocks of marble to the right, left and overhead, shook and fell. More than twenty times over, he was nearly crushed beneath those heavy falls; he certainly would have been if the blue flame, growing, had not enveloped him, when it was necessary, with a diamantine armor, which shattered the blocks without his being scratched. Then, when the danger was past, it was no longer anything more than a little glimmer of gold and azure amid the child's hair.

As he was traversing a clearing in a great forest, a pack of wolves, fur bristling and blood and fire in their eyes, rushed upon him. He could already feel those frightful devouring teeth in his flesh. He got away with a scare. The blue flame, tilting, had dazzled the eyes of the wolves, which fled into the undergrowth howling with fear.

Another time, as he was wading among the rushes of a marsh, a great number of reptiles emerged from the grass and the mud, which coiled around him to choke him; but the little light also became a serpent, like a long lightning-bolt, and the crawling beasts all writhed and died—one might have thought that they were vine branches on a fire—in the blazing rushes.

The child who was traveling toward the Garden of Joy and Dreams escaped many other perils. He soon saw that the fay had not lied, and that nothing could do him any harm as long as the little blue flame was alight. And it did not limit itself to defending him against misfortune and malevolence; it gave him joy in the midst of the most bitter torments. Its light gilded bleak landscapes, but living flowers into all dead brushwood; there was no evening so somber that it did not cheer up with a scattering of stars.

At the same time, the child had a kind of delightful caress that it put on his forehead; he felt his thoughts expanding there as if blossoming, in a radiance, an efflorescence; and his entire soul was aflame, purified and ecstatic, on that divine little pyre.

⁂

One night, the four winds of the four corners of the sky began to blow at the same time. There was a tempest so terrible over the land and the sea that the roofs of the ruined houses flew away, as well as the birds' nests, and the largest ships, their sails torn away and their masts broken, spun in the air like a top under a child's whip. No oak could resist the furious pressure of the gusts. Amid the squalls, enormous cracking sounds could be heard, because of forests laid down the ground more rapidly than grass trampled underfoot. Collapsing mountains slid in torrents of fir-trees and rocks; and the night was black because the tempest had blotted out all the stars.

You can imagine how fearful the child was for the little blue flame. Certainly, paltry as it was, it could not resist the fury of the winds. Taking refuge in a fissure of a mountain that had not yet crumbled, he tried, putting his hands together, to shield it as much as possible from the frantic storm, but a redoubling of the tempest plunged it into the

145

hollows of the rocks; he was knocked over, falling on the stones, unconscious, his forehead bloody.

When he recovered consciousness the next day, he started to weep. What hope could there be that the pretty glimmer had not died in that formidable darkness in which the stars themselves had ceased to shine? But he saw, through the tears, a tremulous reflection of light on a block of marble fallen nearby. O adorable prodigy! He still had the little blue flame on his forehead.

A few weeks later, on a warm June morning, still marching toward the Garden of Joy and Dreams, he was traversing a vast plain in which there was not a single house or tree. He was astonished to perceive, in the distance, near the line of the horizon, something long, dark and smooth, with white patches in places, which gradually advanced, like a living rampart standing out against the sky, in a profound and increasing murmur.

It did not take him long to realize that what was approaching was an enormous mass of water: an inundation whose like had never been seen was invading the plain irresistibly, and the entire region, in an instant, would be nothing more than an immense sea.

The child trembled with fear, not for himself but for his little flame. It would be vanquished by the wave, even though it had triumphed over the wind. He started to flee, running until he was breathless, but in vain. The enormous flood followed him, gaining speed, reached him and bore him away.

For many hours, sometimes swimming and sometimes covered with heavy dampness, he was a wreck rolling in the flow; and when the inundation had reached a burning desert whose sands drank it, when he was lying amid the flowers of an oasis, he sobbed, heartbroken not to have perished—because this time, it was all over, he was sure of no longer having the kindly gleam on his forehead. It must have been extinguished, forever, in the chill of the water.

He uttered a cry of joy. There, in a pool in a hollow in the sand, a gold and azure reflection was trembling. It was still alive, the little blue flame!

From then on he knew the happiness of untroubled hope and certainty. Having repudiated all doubts, he marched proudly to the conquest of his dream. Since the vivacious light had triumphed over the storm and the waves, he was sure of entering the miraculous Garden that opens its diamond gate on the far side of shadow.

⁂

After having traversed all the cities and all the solitudes, after having defied the darkness denser than pitch and conflagrations more furious than a sunset, he stopped, dazzled, because he could finally see, luminous and di-aphanous, the diamantine gate. He had arrived! He was about to penetrate the august paradise of Joy and Dreams. There, he would live eternally happy, having forgotten the sorrows of the obscure world, breathing a subtle air made of the soul of roses and the bright breath of stars; and angelic lilies, in thousands, would be the censers of his glory.

As he hastened his steps, he turned his head because of a little laugh. A young woman, semi-naked on a bed of flowering herbs, made him a sign, showing, in all her plump whiteness, a mouth like a slightly enlarged rose and the tips of her breasts, like two little roses.

147

"Hey, lovely child," she said, "what a pretty blue flame you have on your forehead."

"Yes," he said, "it is pretty."

"Do you know what you would do if you were as courteous and complaisant as it's necessary to be with ladies?"

"What would I do?" he asked.

"You'd let me look at that little gleam at close range; and in return, I'll give you a kiss with my mouth on your forehead. There's nothing more agreeable than the kisses I give."

The child did not see any inconvenience in doing what the semi-naked young woman wanted. What peril was there in allowing that lovely creature devoid of malevolence to admire the invincible light that had triumphed over furious wind and water? He felt sweetly moved because of the hope of the kiss.

He inclined his forehead in order that she could put her mouth thereon, in order that she could gaze at the gold and azure gleam at her ease.

For her part, she drew closer, smiling, opening her rosy lips.

O delightful instant!

But under the young woman's breath during the kiss, the little blue flame went out. And suddenly, the traveler was enveloped by a profound darkness.

And for many years he has been lamenting, groping his way, bumping into invisible walls, falling into unanticipated precipices. And he will never rediscover the route to the incomparable Garden.

MARTINE AND HER ANGEL

IN those days, in that land, there was a child of fifteen named Martine, who was on the point of rendering her soul. The malady had gripped her suddenly; now she was about to die. Her parents, poor country folk who possessed nothing other than an old thatched cottage in the middle of a meager field, experienced a cruel affliction, for they loved the pretty moribund tenderly. The mother, especially, was in despair, firstly because she was her mother, and secondly because, the cottage being a long way from the village, she feared that the parish priest might not arrive before Martine died. Very devout, she wept at the thought that her daughter might cease to live without being confessed and without have received absolution.

"In that regard, have no fear, Madame," said a voice so soft that the parents, in spite of their dolor, were enchanted on hearing it.

At the same time, looming up behind the dying girl's bed, they saw a slightly vague white form, with wings. The voice went on:

"I'm Martine's guardian angel, and I think an angel can replace a priest without any disadvantage. Go into that corner over there and don't turn your heads. Your child will tell me her sins; as she's entirely innocent, it will only take a moment."

It does not often happen that a young girl confesses to an angel, but it happened on that occasion in that country. Martine had soon confessed her slightest peccadilloes; the divine messenger was about to bless her and pardon her, not with his hands but with his wings, when she remembered a big sin that she had committed the previous week. Envious of a pretty neckerchief in pink silk that a neighbor had shown her she had stolen it in order to take possession of it: a double crime, coquetry and larceny. The angel was perplexed.

"I don't know," he said, "whether I ought to absolve you from such a sin. Where is this kerchief?"

"Under the pillow, my good angel."

"It's necessary to return it."

"Oh, willingly, but can I? Ill as I am, I can't take a step or get out of bed, and the neighbor's house is on the other side of the little wood."

"That doesn't matter," said the guardian angel, who had an answer for everything. "Let's make a trade, temporarily. Give me your illness, and take my good health; I'll stay in the bed while you take the kerchief back. Your parents won't notice anything; I'll hide my wings under the bedclothes.

"I'll do as you wish," said Martine.

"But above all, don't waste any time on the way. Imagine what would happen if the moment appointed for your death arrived before you returned; I'd have to die in your place, which would be extremely unbecoming, as I'm immortal."

"Have no fear, my angel! I wouldn't expose you to such a great misfortune. A few minutes will suffice for me to go and come back."

With that, feeling as well as it is possible to be, she leapt out of bed, got dressed in haste, silently, in order not to attract the attention of her parents. When they turned round they saw a sweet pale face on the pillow, with blonde hair; it was the angel, of course, who was hiding his wings under the bedclothes.

⁕⧉⁕

Running through the branches, jumping the ditches, Martine applied all possible diligence. Although it was already pitch dark, she knew the way too well for there to be the slightest risk of going astray. She arrived without delay at the neighbor's house, went in without knocking, slipped the pink silk kerchief into a dresser—fortunately, there was no one at home—and set out to retrace her steps.

To tell the truth, she walked a little less quickly than before. Was she hesitating, now that it was time to return to her angel the health that he had lent her? Not at all. She was very grateful to him for what he had done to ensure the eternal salvation of a poor girl, and was determined to keep her promise. No, certainly not—she would not let him die in her stead! If she was not running, at present, it was because of fatigue. Then again, a nightingale was singing in the nocturnal branches, all silvery with moonlight, and what is sweeter than listening to that song at night? She was hearing it, alas, for the last time.

At the same time, a sadness came over her on thinking that there would be a moonlit and starry sky tomorrow,

151

which she would not see. It was frightful, that bed so close by, where she would sleep forever. But she shook off such cowardly regrets. She launched herself forwards, and she could already perceive in the shadows the old thatched cottage in the middle of the field when the music of a violin became audible in the distance. People were dancing out there, in the hangar of a farm.

She had stopped. She listened, troubled.

She told herself that it was very close by, that farm, and that one waltz—a very little waltz—doesn't last long. Nothing was worse, doubtless than making the angel wait, who was suffering for her, but after all, perhaps the hour when she was to die wasn't as near as everyone thought . . .

⁂

After one waltz, there was another waltz, another, and yet another. Before each one, Marine thought: *The last one, and then I'll go to die.* The music recommenced; the child did not have the strength to leave.

When midnight chimed, however, she gathered all her courage. She would not stay another minute! She would take her place again in the mortuary bed.

As she was leaving the ball, she found herself confronted by a young man so handsome that she had never dreamed that his like could exist. And he was not a peasant, nor one of the nobles from the nearby castle, but the King himself, who, returning that night from a hunt during which he had gone astray with a few courtiers, had called a halt outside the farm in order to see how the country folk amused themselves.

152

At the sight of Martine, he was dazzled; he had never admired at court any princess as lovely as that country girl; and he went very pale, while she went very pink. After a silence, in which they finished becoming infatuated with one another to a degree that is indescribable, the King did not hesitate to proclaim that his heart was fixed forever, and that he would have no other life but that exquisite shepherdess. He ordered that she should be brought to the carriage, where she would take her place in order to come to court.

Alas, Martine, deliciously moved, could not help climbing into the royal carriage; at the same time, she had a very heavy heart, thinking about the guardian angel who was dying in her room, and might perhaps be dead now.

✺ᴖᴖᴖ✺

She was a queen; she had marvelous palaces, and the joy of fêtes, and the glory of being the most illustrious person, with the pride of being the most beautiful. But what delighted her most of all was not the praises of chamberlains and ambassadors; it was not walking of carpets of silk and gold, of wearing dresses flowery with all roses and constellated with all diamonds; no, it was the still vibrant, still increasing amour that burned in her heart for the King, and which burned in the King's heart for her. They experienced an unparalleled affection for one another.

In all the vast world, they did not see anything but one another. Affairs of State were the least of their concerns; they had no other desire but to be left to adore one another in peace; and during their reign no war was made, so busy were they in making love.

153

In the midst of such joy, did Martine think about the celestial messenger who had taken her place out of pure charity? Rarely. Her happiness did not leave her time for that chagrin. And if, sometimes, a pang of remorse came to her for not having kept her promise, she liberated herself from it by telling herself that perhaps Martine, in her thatched cottage, had not been as ill as it appeared, and that the angel might have been cured.

In any case, she scarcely worried about that past, so obscure and so distant, and could not possibly be sad, since she went to sleep every evening with her head on the shoulder of her royal husband.

But something terrible happened: the King disappeared one day, never to reappear, and no one could discover what had become of him.

✻☙❧✻

As soon as she was alone, as soon as she was unhappy, Martine remembered the angel who had waited for her in vain. When one is plaintive, one is inclined to pity. She reproached herself bitterly for having condemned that merciful immortal to death—for he had doubtless ceased to exist a long time ago—and one day, having put on the costume of a pauperess, clothes like the ones she had worn of old, she went toward the cottage in the middle of the field.

Did she hope that there was still time to resume her place in the fatal bed? Oh, no, she knew full well that she had committed an irreparable sin; but she wanted to see again, as a repentant pilgrim, the place where he who had exposed himself to the risk of death for her had suffered.

154

The cottage was no more than rubble in the fallow field. On seeking information from the neighbors, who certainly did not recognize her, Martine learned that the inhabitants of the dwelling that was now a ruin had quit the land long ago after the death of a cherished child, and no one knew where they had gone. As for the child, she was buried in the little cemetery on the hillside.

Thus it was certain, the celestial replacement had died at the moment when she was due to die, and she would have been buried if he had not been buried instead. At least she would go to pray on the angel's tomb.

She went into the cemetery, and knelt down before a low cross on which the name *Martine* could be read among the tall flowering grass. How her heart ached! How culpable she judged herself! With what sobs she implored divine clemency!

But a voice spoke to her, a voice so soft that, in spite of her dolor, she was enchanted on hearing it.

"Don't distress yourself, Martine; things haven't turned out as badly as you might believe."

At the same time, she saw a white, slightly vague form loom up behind the cross, with wings. The voice went on:

"I'm your guardian angel, and all is well, since you're here. Hasten to lie down under this stone, and I'll take your soul to paradise, in order to espouse it there."

"Alas, my good angel, how much you must have suffered, by my fault, in dying, and how tedious you must have found it, alone for such a long time in that grave!"

"Well," he said, "I suspected that you wouldn't come back very soon, and I had taken my precautions in consequence. A vain form deceived your parents, under the bedclothes, on the pillow. I followed you through the branches, and during the time when I ought to have been asleep in your place in the grave, under the flowering glass . . ."

"Oh! During that time, where were you, my angel?"

"I was in our royal palace, my Queen, where you loved me almost as much as you will love me in a little while in Paradise."

THE LAST FAY

O NE day, in a caleche made of a cob-nut shell and
harnessed to four ladybirds, the fay Oriane—who
was no larger than the nail of a little finger—was returning to the forest of Broceliande, where she had the custom of living with her peers. She was coming back from
the baptism of three robins, which had been celebrated in
the hollow of a wall overgrown with wisteria; the fête had
been very pleasant in the nest under the leaves; the pretty
cries of the new-born birds moving their pink wings, almost devoid of down, had permitted the hope that the
fay's godchildren would be excellent singers one day.

Oriane was, therefore, in a very good mood, and as
joy makes one benevolent, she rendered services along the
road to all the people and things she encountered, stuff-
ing clusters of mulberries into the baskets of children going to school, blowing, in order to help them blossom,
on eglantine buds, and putting oats out of the reach of
dewdrops, for fear that mites might drown in them while
passing through them. Two peasant lovers were embracing in a field where the green wheat scarcely came up to
their ankles; she made the sheaves grow and ripen so that
no one could see their kisses from the road. And as, in
doing the good that joy counsels one to do, one becomes

even more joyful, the fay Oriane was, at that point, so full of pleasure that, if she had not feared tipping the carriage over, she would have started to dance in the nutshell.

Soon, however, it was no longer the time to be content. Alas, what had happened? She had been quite sure of following the correct route, but there, where the forest of Broceliande had stirred in the breeze the enchanted mysteries of its profound verdures, there was no longer anything but a vast plain, with scattered buildings, beneath a sky soiled by black smoke.

What has become of you, green and gilded clearing where one danced by starlight, thickets of roses, bushes blooming with thorns, grottoes where slumber smiled on golden moss, in the perfumes and music, and you, subterranean palaces with walls of crystal, which a thousand chandeliers of living gems illuminate on days of celebration? What has become of you, Urgade, Urgèle, Alcine, Viviane and Hulda the pagan,[1] and Melusine the charmer, and you Melandre, Ariel, and you too, Mab and Titania?

"It's in vain that you will call them, poor Oriane," said a lizard that paused in its flight between the stones. "Humans have flooded in great number over your dear solitudes; in order that houses could be built, in order to open a passage for frightful machines breathing vapors and flames, they have felled the trees, burned the rose-thickets and thorn-bushes, filled your mysterious crystal palaces with the stones of your grottoes, and all the fays

1. *Holde la païenne* [Hulda the pagan] refers to the French name of a character in one of the Brothers Grimm's *märchen*, there known as Frau Holle. The epithet is added because scholars have argued that the character had formerly been a Teutonic goddess relegated to a lower status in folklore following the Christianization of the German lands.

have succumbed in the disasters, beneath the collapses. I saw Habonde,[1] who was about to escape, die with a little scream under the foot of a passer-by, like a cricket one crushes."

On hearing that, Oriane began weeping bitterly over the fate of her dear companions, and over her own destiny too; for truly, it was a very melancholy thing to be the only fay left in the world.

What would she do? Where would she hide? Who would defend her against the fury of wicked humans?

The first idea that occurred to her was to flee, no longer to be in that sad place where her sisters had perished. But she could not travel by carriage, as was her custom; the four ladybirds, which she had always treated so well, having heard what the lizard said, had just taken flight, with the ingratitude of all winged creatures. That was a hard blow for the unhappy Oriane, all the more so because there was nothing she detested more than walking. She resigned herself to it, however, and set forth, taking small steps, amid grass that was taller than she was.

She had resolved to go to the home of the robins of the wall overgrown with wisteria; the mother and father of her godchildren would not fail to give her a good welcome; their nest would be a refuge, at least until autumn.

One does not go as quickly with tiny limbs, as in a cobnut shell drawn by the good God's flying creatures. Three long days went by before she perceived the overgrown wall; you can imagine how weary she was. But she would finally be able to rest.

---

1. Dame Habonde, who appears in the Medieval allegory *Roman de la Rose*, is thought by some scholars to be a derivative of the Roman goddess Abundantia, a personification of prosperity.

"It's me," she said, as she approached, "it's me, the fay godmother; come take me, good birds, on your wings and carry me to your abode of moss."

No response; not even a little robin head emerging from the leaves to see who was there. And on widening her eyes, Oriane saw that someone had attached to the wall, in the place where the nest was, a piece of white faience, traversed by the wire of a telegraph line.

As she was going away, not knowing what would become of her, she saw a woman who was carrying in her arms a basket full of wheat and pushing the door of a barn in order to go in.

"Oh, Madame," she said, "if you keep me with you and protect me, you won't have reason to repent of it; fays, like goblins, understand better than anyone how to sort out the good grain from the nasty rye-grass and winnow it, even without a basket. Truly, you would have a very useful servant in me, who would save you a good deal of trouble."

The woman did not hear, or pretended not to hear; she pushed the door open completely and threw the contents of her basket under the cylinders of a machine that winnowed the wheat without there being any need for goblins of fays.

A little further on, on the bank of a river, Oriane encountered men who were standing still around enormous bales, and there was a ship near the bank. She thought that the men did not know how to embark their merchandise.

"Oh, Messieurs," she said, "if you keep me with you and protect me, you won't have reason to repent of it. I'll summon robust gnomes to your aid, who can leap even

with burdens on their shoulders; they'll soon have transported all these heavy things. Truly, you would have a very
useful servant in me, who would save you a great deal of
trouble."

They did not hear her, or pretended not to hear her;
a huge iron hook was lowered, plunging into one of the
bales, and after a half-turn in mid-air, the latter settled gently on the deck of the ship, without the involvement of
any gnome.

As the day wore on, the little fay saw two men through
the open door of a tavern who were playing cards, leaning
over a table; because of the increasing obscurity, it was
becoming very difficult for them to make out the figures
and the colors.

"Oh, Messieurs," she said, "if you keep me with you
and protect me, you won't have reason to repent of it. I
can summon to this room all the glow-worms that light
up on the edges of woods; before long you'll be able to
see clearly enough to continue your game with all possible
pleasure. Truly, you would have a very useful servant in
me, who would save you a great deal of trouble."

The gamblers did not hear her, or pretended not to
hear her; one of them made a sign, and three great jets of
light sprang out of three iron spikes toward the ceiling,
illuminating the whole inn, much better than three thousand glow-worms could have done.

Then Oriane could not help weeping, understanding
that men and women had become too knowledgeable to
have any need of a little fay.

But the next day, she began to hope again. That was
because of a young woman who was dreaming, leaning on
her window-sill, while watching swallows in flight.

It's certain, Oriane thought, *that the people of this world have invented many extraordinary things, but in the triumph of their science and their power, that can't have renounced the eternal and sweet pleasure of amour. I've been very foolish not to have thought of that sooner.*

And, speaking to the young woman at the window, the last fay said:

"Mademoiselle, I know a young man in a distant country more beautiful than the day, whom, without your ever having see him, you love tenderly. He isn't the son of a king or the son of a rich man, but blond curls give him a crown of gold and he holds infinite treasures of tenderness for you in his heart. If you consent, I can bring him to you before very long, and you'll be, thanks to him, the happiest person who has ever existed."

"That's a fine promise you're making me there," said the young woman, astonished.

"I'll keep it, I assure you."

"But what are you asking of me in exchange for such a service?"

"Oh, almost nothing," said the fay. "Let me curl up—I'll make myself even smaller than I am now in order not to inconvenience you—in one of the dimples that a smile puts at the corner of your mouth."

"As you please! It's a bargain."

The young woman had scarcely finished than Oriane, no large than an almost-invisible pearl, was already nestling in the pretty pink nest. Oh, how comfortable she was there! How nice it would be, always. Now, she no longer regretted that humans had devastated the forest of Broceliande; and immediately—for she was too content to neglect to keep her word—she brought the young man more beautiful than the day from the distant country. He appeared in the room, crowned with golden curls, and knelt down before his beloved, with infinite treasures of tenderness in his heart.

But at that moment, a very ugly, aged individual appeared, with gummed-up eyes and a slack lip; he was carrying, in an open casket, a million in precious stones. The young woman ran to him, embraced him, and kissed him so passionately on the mouth that poor little Oriane died, asphyxiated, in the dimple of her smile.

OTHER SNUGGLY BOOKS YOU WILL ENJOY...

DAVID RIX
A Suite in Four Windows

JEAN LORRAIN
Nightmares of an Ether-Drinker

JEAN LORRAIN
The Soul Drinker and Other Decadent Fantasies

JUSTIN ISIS (EDITOR)
Marked To Die, A Tribute to Mark Samuels

KRISTINE ONG MUSLIM
Butterfly Dream

YARROW PAISLEY
Mendicant City

QUENTIN S. CRISP
Rule Dementia!

LÉON BLOY
The Tarantulas' Parlor and Other Unkind Tales

LADY DILKE
The Outcast Spirit and Other Stories

BRENDAN CONNELL
Clark

VICTOR JOLY
The Unknown Collaborator and Other Legendary Tales

FREDERICK ROLFE
The Ossuary of the North Lagoon and Other Stories

9 781943 813254